Müge İplikçi

Mount Qaf

T0106646

Translated by Nilgün Dungan

Milet Publishing
Smallfields Cottage, Cox Green
Rudgwick, Horsham, West Sussex
RH12 3DE England
info@milet.com
www.milet.com
www.milet.co.uk

First English edition published by Milet Publishing in 2014

Copyright © Milet Publishing, 2014

ISBN 978 1 84059 854 4

All rights reserved

First published in Turkish as *Kafdağı* in 2008

Funded by the Turkish Ministry of Culture and Tourism TEDA Project

Printed and bound in Turkey by Ertem Matbaası

Müge İplikçi was born in Istanbul. She graduated from the English Language and Literature Department, Istanbul University, and received MA degrees in women's studies from Istanbul University and Ohio State University. She made her mark at a young age, winning the prestigious Yaşar Nabi Nayır Young Author Award in 1996. She has since published four short story collections and three novels, as well as two books of nonfiction. İplikçi is a member of the Writers in Prison Committee of Turkish PEN, and she has been the chairperson of the PEN Turkish Women Writers Committee since 2007. Her short story "A Question" appears in English translation in *Istanbul in Women's Short Stories*, published by Milet.

Nilgün Dungan is a lecturer and translator based in İzmir. She studied English language and literature at Ege University and received an MA in management from Bowie State University in Maryland. She is currently pursuing her PhD in translation studies at Boğaziçi University, Istanbul and teaching in the Department of English Translation and Interpreting, İzmir University of Economics. Her English translations of short stories are featured in *Istanbul in Women's Short Stories* and in various journals and magazines. She is Assistant Editor of *Aeolian Visions/Versions: Modern Classics and New Writing from Turkey*, also published by Milet, and seven translations by her are featured in the book.

Guide to Turkish Pronunciation

Turkish letters that appear in the book and which may be unfamiliar are shown below, with a guide to their pronunciation.

c   as *j* in *just*

ç   as *ch* in *child*

ğ   silent letter that lengthens the preceding vowel

ı   as *a* in *along*

ö   as German *ö* in *Köln*, or French *œ* in *œuf*

ş   as *sh* in *ship*

ü   as German *ü* in *fünf*, or French *u* in *tu*

Müge İplikçi

Mount Qaf

1

It was a night in the past when everything shuddered to a halt, a night that was the end of all.

That's how she began to tell me her story. A woman couldn't easily reveal such kinds of secrets to a man. But what can we call such a life? Was it nothing more than a yellow file filled with envelopes? That file turned out to be her destiny. After a while, I stopped asking irrelevant questions and simply listened. I've been told that I'm a kind criminologist. That very well may be so. Confronted with Zahide Sohni Mühür's story, I decided to remain silent. Zahide, or Sohni as she was called when we first met, appeared in my life just after I'd undertaken a rather long journey. That was in Istanbul, just before I'd decided to continue working in Turkey for a short while, rather than in the United States. On those mornings when I looked at her through the sleepy eyes of my own city, she told her story, fragmented, crazed and weary, reflected from her past into the present. Over time, I began losing track of the paths and traces weaving through her mind. In those days, she was kept drugged all the time. There was no way I could have known where that adventure would lead me, that I would experience so much and more. Our first encounter was in a stadium. Yes, a stadium. That's where she was living. She'd resigned herself to her enslavement, and beyond that, nothing really mattered. Dressed in orange, she approached and as she sat opposite me, I could hear the clinking of her chains. Occasionally, the horns of the ferryboats would merge with the blare of train whistles. She said that the past was as close to her as a pane of glass. If she were to hold it there, so close. Blow upon its surface. That's what she said.

Those were her words. I was merely a witness.

She had two sons, İzzet and Ahmet, who was the older of the two. They slept in different rooms. İzzet's room overlooked the yard and trees, which in the night would take on shapes under the glow of light from the neighbor's houses. One night at around two o'clock in the morning, İzzet called for his mother. Mom, come here, he said. He nestled deeper into his pillow. Zahide put her own pillow at the foot of his narrow bed. Sleep now, İzzet, she pleaded. Sleep, please go to sleep. Okay Mom, he said. Under the glow of the lights of the other houses, as the ghost of the lights flitted among the trees, he fell asleep. Zahide waited quietly, holding her breath. She had already been awake for hours.

Then, somewhere between wakefulness and sleep, she heard a sound like horseshoes. But it was nothing new; since the day before, she'd been hearing them. That clip-clop reminded her of horses, the sound of the hooves of the horses pulling carriages past the house where she lived as a young girl. No, she thought, these sound freer, lighter; it's probably just a deer. The leaps and bounds seemed timorous, unsure, prone to a misstep. It must be a deer lost in the night, she decided. She listened to İzzet's breathing. He was sleeping the sound sleep of a child. When she lifted her head from the pillow, Zahide saw clouds drifting past in the sky. Driven by the night wind, they descended all the way down to the windowsill through the open curtain. Then she watched the play of lights glimmering like an enchanted recital among the wet branches of a tree, which she thought must be a slender pine. As the wind shook free the rainwater that had gathered on the branches, the lights from the neighbor's house were scattered in a shower of droplets. The sound of the deer's footsteps mingled with the mist of early dew clinging to the pine tree.

İzzet slept. The lights slept.

She knew they would come in the morning to take her away. She listened to the sound of the deer. She wasn't sure why, but she was most troubled by thoughts of İzzet. Reasoning with herself, she came to the conclusion that it couldn't be seen as such a shocking crime. After making sure that İzzet was fast asleep, she went into Ahmet's room. He was asleep as well, breathing deeply. Then she went around the house, closing everything that was open. She closed every single gap, one by one, so there would be no record of their lives once they were gone. Then she prayed; an early morning prayer for the slightest shadow that could fall across their souls, and then she prayed for the slightest shadow that could fall over her, for all the shadows of the past and the future.

The message was clear: Leave no trace behind. It seemed pointless to delve into the details of such a statement. No, there was no problem. Zahide had learned quite well how to discipline her body. She knew how to separate her body from her soul. It seemed that the moment that she had been awaiting for two years had finally arrived. The moment when she would swear to leave behind no trace except for her silent memories in that house.

She went to the gas stove and turned on all four burners. Like a cat stretching, gas filled the kitchen. She put on her jacket which she always wore when she went out. Covering her hair, she caressed the heads of her sleeping children.

For the last time.

At first she had to hold back her tears. Soon enough, however, she had calmed down. Everything burns, leaving not a trace behind, she murmured to herself. Then, in the dark of the morning, she laid down on the sofa bed in the living room of that house where she'd been living for the past two years.

The chill of early morning seeping through the living room windows sent a shiver through her. I should have closed the windows better, she thought. But her body was growing weaker and weaker, until she couldn't move a muscle. She was on the cusp of a painless, eternal journey with her sons.

At that point, Zahide began to understand that time is nothing but a collection of moments that never seem to end in the chill of morning, that threats could be snatched from the deepest recesses of a person's very being, and that when an ember falls, that's the place it burns the most. For the first time, she understood this quite clearly.

In that cloud of gas filling the air, her children were dying. And Zahide was their killer. That burden was unbearable. She was their angel of death, shoving open the gates of heaven. But in fact, at that moment, she was like a stone lodged on a mountain. Not a mother who brings her children face to face with death, but a stone in the mountains, long forgotten.

As she sank into the deep folds of weariness, she would realize that she was murmuring a song to herself.

God, take us into your Heaven.

2

"What exactly do you mean by 'the program'?"

Keeping to the terms and conditions of the Pont journalism scholarship I'd been awarded, that's the question I asked the senator sitting across from me, who actually helped fund the grant. I planned on using that interview for a report I had to submit at the end of the program. We were talking about the rendition program involving Muslims taken into custody by the US government. Those people were then flown overseas and imprisoned in countries which served as subcontractors. The authorities would then do to those people whatever they thought seemed permissible under the tenets of democracy, even though they hadn't been convicted of a crime. The whole business was mired in questions, yet no one, except for a few people in Hollywood, seemed to care. I was tasked with discussing the topic with someone determined by the administrative office to be an authority on the matter.

It was one of those sunny winter days in Washington, DC, typical of its landlocked climate. I'd been there for ten days, and there was much I needed to do. For one thing, I hadn't been able to find a proper place at the guesthouse; rents downtown were quite expensive, and living in the suburbs struck me as being nothing short of succumbing to death. On top of that, it seemed increasingly likely that chilly weather was moving our way. Despite the cold, however, ashes from hell continued raining down upon the earth, and I pushed forward with my work on journalism, which seemed to me to be the best way to further stoke the flames of hell. That's what had brought me there, and as a result I found myself having to learn the academic aspects of the field of journalism. On the surface, that was a time for me to come to terms with myself and my life. However, there was also an emotional dimension to this which was anchored in the past: I applied for the scholarship in the hopes that I would be able to get away from Istanbul, even if just for a short while, and erase from my memory the traces of death that lurked in my thoughts. I'd lost both my husband and my son in the Gölcük earthquake of 1999. We'd gone to Adapazarı to attend my sister's traditional henna night celebration before her wedding just a day before the quake struck, and that was the end of it all. I lost everyone in my family. It was as if I'd buried my soul along with them. Intensive drug treatment followed sessions of therapy. But then I woke up one day. It was like the rebirth of someone who had died long before. I didn't know why exactly, but I felt a need to live. In time I would understand that this was atonement, the kind that follows such incidents. Living became a conscious effort for me, one that I took up for the sake of the people I had lost. I needed to find an answer, a way out of the feeling that I was falling apart, and in the meantime I so desperately struggled with all my own worldly sins and good deeds. And yet, contrary to what you might expect, this was not an answer that held some sort of divine meaning. It was rooted in the kind of language you need to respond to the attitudes of the age by speaking on its own terms. A corpse wandering about in the barrenness of life had risen to its feet. That was me, but I knew it was impossible to understand the person I had become. I was new, I was unknown, and there were multiples of me. I didn't recognize myself; I couldn't, it seemed beyond my grasp. Losing your loved ones overnight could at best become a feeling that, after years of building up your strength and immunity, you could finally discuss with yourself. Your life is not your own if you cannot speak to yourself about it, and mine was suffused with a feeling of alienation. I had worn my new life like a straitjacket and accepted it as the bare minimum. Beyond that was time, a time in which I didn't believe and cared little for.

I was, in fact, caught up in a bizarre whirlpool, one that I could say consisted of escape and pursuit. If you ask why, despite all those plans of escape I wasn't just lost in memories of my family; no, there was yet another memory that I pursued, and that was Zahide. For years I had been in pursuit of her. I'd begun looking for her, for no apparent reason, while I was searching for myself. A feeling of indebtedness I had established with life once again, and the feeling that followed, suddenly put Zahide by my side on the strange path that I set out on. Whatever I was, so was she. For reasons inexplicable to me, she was me and I was her; she was lost, so was I. It was as if Zahide had disappeared without a trace, and I had, too. We didn't exist, she didn't exist. Her children were dead, but I knew she wasn't. I'd found out that she was a victim of the rendition program, and was captured and wounded when her house, which was under surveillance, was raided. I also found out that she was later whisked out of the country on planes secretly registered to the CIA. The rest was a complete mystery. My curiosity grew with her absence. And, as I told myself, nothing was impossible as long as there was curiosity. My search for her had been ongoing for some time. I'd felt that fatigue, call it getting older or what you will, but I'd found no sign of her. It seemed that all the rivers of answers in the world had dried up. But I felt deep down that if I found her, I would also find a part of myself. It was a reunion I had a hard time explaining even to myself. In the end, I decided to follow my doctors' orders and focus more on the results than the reasons. Whatever they were, I was determined to find Zahide.

Before I arrived in DC with the Pont journalism scholarship, which would fund my stay there for several months, I made sure that I secured the approval of the newspaper where I worked in Istanbul to investigate the story. But that was relatively meaningless, in any case, since Pont stipulated that I could only publish the story after completing the period of the scholarship and submitting my report on the topic I chose. On top of that, we weren't allowed to publish the report in full. In short, it was clear to me that the matter would come to a dead end because of the statute of limitations and ultimately, the public would more or less remain in the dark about what was going on. Nonetheless I persisted, because I knew that for Zahide, and others like her, time is nothing but a grain of sand in the grand scheme of the universe. Whatever that meant for the dead, it was the same for those who were lost.

That had all gone through my mind within a short period of time. As I sat across from the senator, I must have looked like I'd drifted in and out of another dimension, as I found myself suddenly confronted with the question, "Are you following what I'm saying, Emel?"

"Ofcourseofcourse," I said, my answer rattling off like a machine gun.

But he was right to ask me that. My feeling of being lost wasn't just tied to that particular moment.

Since the beginning of our conversation, I found my gaze occasionally lingering on the bags under his eyes as he talked with surprising frankness, albeit with language laced with irony. His long, thin, mottled fingers which flitted in the air, terminated in long nails that made his fingers seem even longer. I thought to myself, simply watching this porcelain-toothed man and his facial expressions could be a game in itself. The backdrop of our conversation, which indeed unfolded like a game, was a panoramic view of the Capitol towering over green grass.

"They call this rendition," replied the senator. He had headed the intelligence committee at the White House for several years. He was ageing but still quite fit, and a bit of a flirt as well.

"What kind of rendition is it?"

An insincere smile tugged at his lips.

"Frankly, I'm surprised that you, as a Turkish journalist, have never heard of it."

"Of course I have. I know about it. However, I have my doubts about the reason why it's called rendition and not torture, and I need you to confirm that distinction in your own words."

"Of course we can't call it torture. As you well know, our modern age is not exactly one of complete honesty. There's no need to stir up any trouble. All you do is pick people up and then put them on trial."

"You call that a trial?"

"Of course I do."

"What exactly do you mean by a trial, Mr. Senator?"

"Look, you're fairly familiar with Americans aren't you? Correct me if I'm wrong."

"I can't say that I am."

"Well, surely you know a little about their principle of, let's say, flexibility and discretion in politics."

"I suppose."

"Okay, then you should also know that we're not going to make the same mistakes made by President Clinton in terms of US foreign policy. We simply can't condone the deaths of hundreds of civilians. And, on this point, please don't give me the typical third-world response by bringing up the example of Iraq."

"That was never my intent."

"Ah, you see? Now here's a woman who knows what's what."

"It's just that . . ."

"Please allow me to finish."

"Go right ahead."

"Of course, capturing a dictator shouldn't involve the killing of civilians. In the process, however, you can't expect the CIA to predict the future."

"But in most places and for many people, the ordinary rules did not, and do not, work. Picking people up and trying them, in your words, or to put it more bluntly, sending them off on planes to remote corners of the world and torturing them there . . ."

"Look, my dear Emel . . . May I call you Emel?"

"Sure."

"I'm very glad we got to meet. When Pont contacted me, I frankly didn't expect anyone like you. How should I put it? You aren't uptight. But you tend to get a bit emotional about things. For example, that Pakistani woman, what did you say her name was?"

"Zahide."

"Right, Zahide. In such cases, the CIA doesn't have the means to look into everything on a case-by-case basis. Do you see what I mean? So you say this woman was picked up from her home in a raid, then brought to Dulles and put into a secret witness protection program run by the FBI and Pakistani secret service, and so on. How could that have happened, and where is she now? I have no way of knowing all that, honestly. After all, the CIA is a state institution too."

"But wasn't it you who said, at the beginning of our conversation, that it is unethical to disclose the most secret programs of the CIA?"

"That's exactly what I'm saying, Emel, we're taking about a sacred organization here. It's the lifeblood of the country. Now if we were to put everything out in the open like that, people would just be over-whelmed. There's no need to give out a lot of information or go into detail about where these planes take off and land. But I can say this much, one of the places where these planes are refueled, and listen carefully here, where the detainees in the rendition program are put on the planes is the Incirlik Base in Turkey. Am I making myself clear?"

"No," I said.

"No? Good God, why not? Oh, I see. You're still being emotional about all this. Perhaps you're right. But I can't help you beyond that point. As I said, I can tell you that this rendition business involves nothing but putting people on trial by following the established procedures. That's all I can say, Emel. Anything more than that would run contrary to our policy of the 'future is ours,' and that, in fact, is America's objective. Our country simply can't afford to do that. And, oh, the mistakes . . . Of course mistakes have been made and will be made. Remember Operation Goldenrod. Just look at what President Reagan said about that operation."

"What did he say?"

"I'll tell you if you'll give me a chance! He said that for such operations they had to use rendition against terrorists. And the Department of Justice made a critical statement about that subject in 1988 when the decision was made to allow the CIA and FBI to apprehend terrorists in countries like Lebanon. What's more, this decision was made not only by the United States, as you might guess. Now, that's the precise point where we can easily articulate rendition."

"How do we do that?"

"Do what?"

"Articulate rendition?"

"We can explain r-e-n-d-i-t-i-o-n as the practice of arresting a criminal (here he raises his voice) and bringing them to the United States."

"Why do you think such a decision was made?"

"Well, before that, you couldn't arrest your target even if you'd been able to corner them. Do you know what that means? Releasing criminals back onto the streets where they came from. However, the rendition program eliminated all these difficulties. It's clean business. Plain, clear, diplomatic relations. Who can say anything about that?"

"But it's a broad net, you pull in the good along with the bad."

"Look, look, please . . . I'm not saying that mistakes have never been made. What's important is being able to distinguish correct decisions from the wrong. After all, we are a country with a mature tradition of democracy, so we can't legitimize something we don't find appropriate. Don't worry yourself about that. I hope I didn't mislead you by what I've said. I'd never want that. But if we want to combat terrorism, we need to know that the problem can't be eliminated only with secret operations. We need plainer, open methods. And in doing that, you follow a clear path, one that could even be considered routine. So, who are we after? People who have an arrest warrant out on them."

"Or someone without a warrant . . ."

"Just a moment, hold your judgment. The essence of the rendition program is something quite different. Please allow me to finish. You can apprehend someone who has an arrest warrant out on them in a way that's clearly set out with very specific rules and then arrest them without having to go through the paperwork."

"So what's the basic difference between what's been done in the past and what's being done now when you put someone on trial by law?"

"Well, it's quite simple actually. In the past, any means were justified! Now they're not. You're not going to believe this, but they're not.

Only on one condition. Justice isn't such a major issue anymore with situations like that! In short, the purpose is to get information, not to punish. Intelligence. That's the name of our day and age. The basic reason that we transfer detainees to other countries is the intelligence that these countries will get using their own means."

"I know what you are trying to say. So I guess that kidnapping, torturing and interrogating certain people in the meantime is something quite normal."

"Ah, as I said, should we talk about seeking out an idea of justice, or not? For the rendition program, no. That program has no such goal."

"Should the government of the United States continue in this way to claim that torture is never done on its soil? Do you still think that you're abiding by the Geneva Convention—which your country is a party to—which stipulates that detainees should not be tortured?"

"Frankly, I prefer not to answer that question."

"Wasn't the United States able to put the rendition program into effect thanks to subcontractors, in your opinion?"

"Not exactly. Countries that lend support to the United States can't really be called subcontractors. I suppose you mean countries when you say subcontractor, right?"

"Countries and their secret services . . ."

"Okay then. In that case, let me give you a country for an example. For instance, Afghanistan. That country has its own prisons. It has its own methods of interrogation. If the ultimate goal is to defeat terrorism, we can only tip our hat to that."

"Nevertheless, there are countries like Egypt, too."

"What about Egypt?"

"There, detainees are brought to heel first by local prison officers and then by the CIA."

"That idea is based on completely misguided opinions. You keep forgetting one fact: Terrorism is a danger to us all."

"Well then, what are the grounds of suspicion? Who is a suspect? That's the biggest aberration of the program, as I see it."

"Suspicion? In that respect, we have no choice but to trust the secret services."

"Mr. Senator, we're talking about a system that brings people under suspicion because of contacts in email address lists, am I wrong?"

"Look, Emel, it isn't that simple."

"Some of those prisoners are apprehended and taken away. They are sent from prison to prison. And that goes on for years. They're subjected to horrendous torture. And some of those people are actually innocent."

"There's really not much I can say in this regard. You may think that your Pakistani friend has fallen victim to something like that. But I would say that there is a very slim chance of that."

"But there are examples of that happening. There are people who, even though they are innocent, have been moved around for years in planes chartered by the CIA."

"I'm sorry, Emel, I think you should do what everyone else does. Look at what happened in Guantánamo. Look, I don't say this to everyone. But look at the press releases, what's been written about it. Look at what happened to those people. They get moved from place to place, and on what grounds? You see what I'm saying, don't you? I'm not sure if I can explain this. How have they been moved around? Look at that. In short, don't stand idle. Ha-ha! That's the funny part of it."

"I have one last question for you. I have information indicating that these people are being moved to stadiums in big cities in subcontractor countries, literally packed into such places. That's based on a recent secret law enacted by the Bush administration."

"Stadiums are safe places!"

"In what way?"

"I was just thinking about the case of Chile. Why shouldn't stadiums be the holiest of shelters for our country too! We've used them again and again when disasters strike. At stadiums, you can resolve problems plaguing the population like unfair treatment and disorder. They're safe, open to the outside but closed in as well. Stadiums don't cause any problems."

"You're speaking in riddles."

"Because that's the only way I can talk about this. I'm surprised that you managed to get hold of such information."

"When I said secret, I meant hidden from the American public. Just like anything else, you can get information about these stadiums on the internet. All you have to do is to search the words rendition and stadium together."

"That's what I call transparent administration! Rendition and stadium. I'll try that. But before that, I have a question for you."

"What?"

"Are you doing anything this evening?"

My answer was neither yes nor no. My eyes were fixed on the cloudy sky above the city. Any honorable journalist would have done the same.

3

During our second meeting, Zahide told me about what she went through after she was captured. Her mind would come and go; sometimes she would call me Levent, and at other times, Richard. Occasionally, she would even become delirious, calling me a ghost in a uniform. Initially, our interviews were held in English. But just as her Turkish quickly improved, her memory deteriorated at the same rate. She said that she'd spent her days studying Turkish, and mentioned that her father would have been proud of her accomplishments.

Compared to how she looked at our first meeting, she'd lost a lot of weight, and she'd begun to slur when she spoke. After the raid on her house, she was admitted to a hospital administered by the CIA. After a month of treatment, she was turned over to the rendition program. When she opened her eyes, she found herself in the presence of Karen Blaster, a nurse who also the coordinator of the program that she would have to undergo.

"Zahide Mühür?"

" . . . ?"

"Zahide?"

Light and Zahide . . .

Ever since she closed her eyes, she had been seeing lights that resembled fireflies.

A deer trotted through the night garden and lights were delicately falling far away behind the clouds, like the twinkling of fireworks. Darkness and Zahide . . . Whenever she summoned her eyes back to life to remember, they would fade with resentment, they would pull away in indignation and disappear.

Now, there was a figure dressed in grey and a pair of blue eyes looking at her.

She found herself in a room that was completely white. The weight of her body was palpable. Her joints and bones were stretching and her spirit moved inside her.

But I'm dead, her spirit said.

I set out on a journey to infinity, leaving my body outside of me, it said.

I died.

Yet the person with those blue eyes looked like a nurse. It was an ordinary pair of blue eyes. Normal eyes which showed no signs of magic or otherworldliness.

"Zahide Mühür?"

Zahide felt the nurse's skin brushing against her own.

I died, the spirit inside her said.

You're alive, another voice said. From far away.

You're alive. Your sons are dead, but you're not dead, you're living. You're alive.

It was a dream. An imaginary voice. But such a voice that it even had a smell. It was the kitchen of her childhood, filled with the scent of onion and spices. That was the sound of an onion she'd heard after gazing at the ceramic tiles of the kitchen, tiles she thought were stained with coffee. It was the beautiful sound of the voice of her mother who she saw on the doorstep just beyond the garden.

Mother, you died years ago. The soldiers came to our house late one night and killed you, and then they killed my father in the dungeons. Ziya, meaning light. Lack of light. Ziya-ul-Haq, light of God. God? Light of God, that's what they said. There's a family moving towards the end with him. A father born in Istanbul. Then comes Kashmir Valley. And then a marriage. A history that moves from Kashmir Valley to Karachi and begins to be drenched in blood in that place where she and her siblings were born. A father who told her about Istanbul for years, a father who bequeathed the Turkish words that wandered in his vast memory to his daughter. Then her mother . . . A voice that's the most beautiful sea of Urdu: HER mother, Pervin.

Sohni, this voice says. Sohni, my dear daughter, you're alive. Sohni? She hasn't heard that name in ages. She's always been Zahide.

It's an old childhood memory. She was in a garden. Yet before that, she remembered the kitchen, which opened onto the garden. She dreamed she touched the ceramic tiles with her hands, the bumps she thought were coffee spilt on the white surface. She must have been crawling. Until she was around eighteen months old. That old house. Later, every time she remembered the tiled floor, her mother would say, it's not possible, Sohni, no one remembers anything that far back.

She was eighteen months old and crawling.

Sohni, you're alive.

Sohni remembers well her mother's beautiful face, that moment when her mother was busying herself among the pots and pans in the kitchen. With her bare, chubby legs, Sohni is advancing slowly but eagerly towards the kitchen where her mother is.

At that moment, Sohni notices a long stripe. The stripe glides beside her. Looking closely, Sohni sees that the stripe has eyes and even a green ring around its neck. Of course, the stripe sees her, too. She's a curly-haired baby girl, looking at it with curious eyes. With its profound memory, the black stripe looks at this child whose chubby legs are sprawled on the paving stones of the garden. There's curiosity in Sohni's eyes, and ice in the eyes of the black stripe.

Just as Sohni is about to crawl up onto the step separating the garden from the kitchen, she sniffles. Her mother sees Sohni at the bottom of the steps. And she sees the snake next to her. In Sohni's mind, that is the moment when her mother's face is transformed into two huge black eyes.

For Sohni, or Zahide as she preferred to be called in later years, that memory stopped at that moment. For years, that brief moment was talked about again and again.

That moment when she was eighteen months old, which Zahide truly believes she can remember, entered the Karachi music scene as the song "Sohni Remembered."

Sohni, now Zahide, hears her mother's voice. No, it's more than that; she actually remembers it.

The black snake silently slithers past, not looking at Sohni, not looking at anyone. That same black stripe passes over the doorstep where the steps begin, just before Sohni's mother sees Sohni with the snake and screams. Her mother is about to look up from the onions softening in the oil in the frying pan. And the moment comes. That's when the snake slithers past the left edge of the doorstep. All at once, browning onions, brown tiles, and the black snake fill the pupils of her mother's eyes. Her mother instantly assumes that the snake slithering past was her child's killer.

A very quiet split second. Everything stops. The snake glides from the left edge of the doorstep back into the wild of the garden. Baby Sohni climbs up the step and begins crawling towards her mother. Then the sound of the onions in the oil can be heard. The sound bursts and turns into firecrackers set off during holidays. The onions are now saturated with oil.

That's when Sohni's mother begins shrieking.

Sohni, you're alive . . .

I'm dead, Zahide says. You're mistaken, Mother, I'm dead.

Sohni's mother clasps her in her arms in that kitchen as if seeing her for the first time and throws her up in the air, nibbles her arms, kisses her neck.

Sohni, you're alive, my dear you're alive, her mother says, you're alive.

The face of life—coursing through river basins, smelling of earth, shaping a fresh spirit—is looking at a young mother. The mother is very beautiful at that hour of that day. The dreams of life—moments which could respond if you were to touch them, and from those moments, you slip away into eternity—are very beautiful. Light. This is the image of beauty before it deserted this world, the light that illuminated the mother's face.

Sohni, you're alive.

You're alive.

Life.

Her pulse is normal, says the blue-eyed woman, the nurse, life, the moment. And she shines a lifeless white light into Zahide's eyes. That's when Zahide understands that she has fallen into the middle of the eye-searing light of hell.

Now we can start on your injections, the nurse says. Each injection leaves a sour taste, a taste of hell. Zahide will come to realize that over time. She'll discover that after the first five minutes she forgets but at the same time finds herself flipping through the pages of her memory. After a while, the only thing she'll know is the way the muscular hands of the military nurse—whose name, she finds out, is Karen—grips her thin arm and enters into her life through her veins; the injections begin by numbing her arm, and shortly after, herself, her mind, her soul fall away, beyond the pain of her body.

The blessing of oblivion. Heroes always forget that.

"What should we call you from now on, Zahide?" Karen will ask.

At that time, Zahide will be looking at the room's ceiling, the glow of her eyes not yet extinguished. She'll hear Karen's voice somewhere in her mind as she tries to hear all the other voices. That is the voice of torture, she'll come to understand, but she won't let on that she knows. As the brightness of her mind begins to turn to ice, she'll whisper to Karen.

"Sohni."

For a few minutes, Karen will look pityingly at this Pakistani woman; soon she will be taking a long trip. She'll look at the face of this woman in that brief moment when the sense of duty will replace feelings of sympathy. She needs to keep this woman alive and well, because she will be transported to new tortures on a plane a week later. That's how Karen looks at her. It's the compassion that envelops a victim before she's sacrificed. Compassion left to hang in the air.

"All right, Sohni. Tell us what you remember."

At that very moment, Zahide will say something that seems to take possession of the room.

"I'm the plague of the age."

4

In front of me was an article entitled "Zahide Mühür: The Plague of the Age." I couldn't believe my eyes.

In the morning, I'd attended one of the fifteen courses required by the scholarship, and later I found that article while searching for materials about Zahide in the archives of the library which overlooked the university's vast lawns. At three o'clock I was supposed to meet with Nadir, an Iranian journalist also studying on the same scholarship. Nadir said he knew someone who might be able to help me find a place to rent.

In the meantime it had begun snowing. Snow fell on that article that slandered Zahide, but to no avail . . .

That article, however, would shatter my beliefs about Zahide and her innocence. As the text appeared on the screen before me, I tried to convince myself that my primary goal was to rediscover an old friendship. I soon realized that the style of the article was, in fact, rather amusing. Beyond a doubt, the article invoked strong words with the intent of infusing our day to day lives with a desire for revenge. The main argument centered on an obsessive belief that the world could be cleanly divided into black and white. That theme was shrouded in feelings which you'd somehow recognize for their sharpness, even if you didn't want to acknowledge them. The text surged with a kind of grim determination and wrath that would invariably fall away, however, when faced by the conscience of cutting-edge politics, no matter where in the world you might happen to be. I imagined the author as being the type of person who would quietly sob in a corner at home and then suddenly begin swearing, lashing out in vengeance. It was razor-sharp. But at the same time, that sharpness made the article just as amusing as it was tragic. The stance was so uncompromising that soon enough its inner contradictions began rising to the surface. Any sensible person would have long ago delegated it to the wastebasket of their mind. Not because there are many more important things to do in this world—in fact there are, and you could save that nobility for more serious endeavors—but you could simply forget that article for one simple reason: to have a more peaceful afternoon.

That afternoon was anything but peaceful for me, and I couldn't get that article out of my mind. I struggled to find an explanation for the way I felt, but nothing fully satisfied me. In the end, I decided that I'd entered a period of time in my life in which the world had no time for peaceful afternoons, evenings, sunsets, and mornings. The possibility of Zahide Mühür being an ordinary person was of little comfort. Zahide Mühür could never be the same again. How was it possible that those amusing lines were so suddenly transformed into such a hateful message? What had Zahide Mühür done to become the plague of the times? How could the *Washington Post* publish such a biased article?

Just to the left of the article there was a small photograph of her. Perhaps the parts of her face normally in shadow were a little darker and the lighter parts were a little brighter, but it was Zahide. Her narrow forehead appeared brighter than it did in real life, and the dark circles around her eyes were even darker. In the picture, she was thinner than when I'd known her, and her cheeks seemed to have sunken.

Her nose was a blur, but her chin spoke of great determination. That was the only part of her face that said anything. Her lips were pressed tightly together, as though they'd never parted or uttered a word. It seemed that if she were there with me, she would say:

Just like they're sealed, aren't they?

As a matter of fact, her lips did seem sealed in the photograph. They were quiet, tacit, at a zero point, as if to say that the best response to that accursed article would be the deep breath which could pass between those sealed lips. From that point on, the entire photograph could be said to be a portrait of reticence, spreading from her lips to the rest of her face. Still, her face suggested that she hadn't said everything she'd wanted to but had succumbed to weariness. That wasn't the Zahide I knew; the picture before me was the face of a woman fed up with talking and explaining herself to others. It was difficult to choose a manner which disapproved of all the accusations made against her; this woman's expression was somewhere between self-confidence and utter exhaustion, between endurance and submission. She looked more like someone who set out to be a cure for the plague, rather than being the plague itself, but she seemed indifferent as well.

I don't know how long I stared at that dark, faint picture. Just as I don't know how many times I tried to stitch together that photo with the ideas in the article. Terrorist, bomb, September 11, main mastermind, Al-Qaeda, plane tickets, fundamentalism, precious gems, agents . . . The portrait that emerged with those words suggested that she was one of the faces behind September 11. And to what extent! According to the text, there was practically no end to the horrors carried out by her and her husband. In the statement given by Abu Seyam, who was held in custody as one of the leading terror suspects in America, Zahide's name was listed as one of the most important masterminds behind Al-Qaeda. As a matter of fact, that was when the storm started to break loose. Zahide was put under close surveillance. In the meantime, her past banking transactions were closely examined. Countless times Saudi currency had been deposited in her account before September 11. Zahide's name was also mentioned in relation to diamond shipments from Africa to the United States between 1998 and 2002. It was claimed that she had been an active member of Al-Qaeda as a mentor, intermediary, and advisor, not to mention that it was quite likely that she had the blood-stained hands of a murderer, and so on and so on.

The virulent words that appeared over and over in the article didn't stop there, however. Then there was the FBI, her time under FBI protection, and the assurances of the Pakistani secret service. I knew that she'd been under protection, but until I read that article, I thought it was because of her husband. The article attempted to prove that Zahide was just as guilty as her husband. Such odd arguments would be enough to make you think differently of the person in the photograph. According to the text, Zahide Mühür was initially taken into the witness protection program as an informant. Think of it: she was both exposed as a terrorist by the FBI and then taken into witness protection! Zahide would have had a good laugh with me about that one. At least, if we'd been together on a train, like those days from the past . . . Yet for some reason, I was speechless in the face of that fabrication. And there was more: after she was taken into the program, she'd disappeared one day! According to the article, this proved one singular fact: that she was a double agent. However, neither the FBI nor the Pakistani Secret Service knew her exact whereabouts. That was precisely why she was the plague of the age—that is, of course, according to the article.

I was perplexed. The author, Jan Gabriel, seemed to have worked out his own version of Zahide Mühür. My Zahide Mühür, on the other hand, kept quietly gazing out from the photograph in which she was imprisoned. I felt as though I were trying to buy time. There was nothing I could do but frantically scratch my head as though tearing out my hair.

I was at a complete loss.

It had been years since I'd heard from her. Yet she'd made a promise, saying that she would write to me, keeping her memory alive.

As it was, the past was but a stage without a curtain. The snowy weather and the piercing cold must have had something to do with that feeling. But something seemed to have stirred at that moment, and I was part of that moment, too.

Zahide Mühür . . . Zahide, somewhere in my mind . . . When she was in her twenties, she came to the United States to study and ended up living in a well-off campus city in the Midwest. Ohio State University. It was a Midwest location that wouldn't suit everyone, an archetypical land of colleges; pick any you like of all the universities that turn such huge profits for the country. A green, secluded, quiet city. Zahide Mühür stayed there for seven years. It had been difficult for her to start a new life squeezed between the long hallways of the Faculty of Dentistry and the buildings illuminated with icy blue lights. People dealing with familiar problems would have had an easier time, but Zahide had started running out of patience. We'd met not at the dormitory, where by coincidence we had adjacent rooms, but at the pool. It was 1991. The month of October. The leaves on the trees were turning orange and red. Swimming at the dull campus pool was one way to lighten up life on Friday nights on that campus that stretched for miles on end. After glancing at the clock which was across from the pool, we'd drop seven layers below the earth and with a deep breath, rise seven layers into the air.[1] What could you do about a minute hand that kept postponing its return to its home at twelve, slowing down all the time in the world on its dirty white face? We wanted nothing to do with being the hour hand, nor of being hours. Unraveling the mystery of time was beyond us, and that's why we continued to swim strokes in the chlorinated water.

And that's when I drowned. At least that's how it seemed to me . . .

I had moved there to get my master's degree. In the fall semester, I had to submit a proposal for my thesis and get it approved. At the time, I hadn't even written a decent line yet, and my advisor turned out to be quite difficult to get along with. Of course, that could happen to anyone. When Zahide and I were talking about it, that's what she told me and then laughed, and we decided that the real reason for my drowning—I didn't actually drown, I was just within moments of drowning—was not water. The problem was breathing. In a nutshell, it was about me. Zahide told me that the key to breathing was related to understanding life. There was nothing romantic at all about what she said; she was more like a coach, a confident and coolheaded coach, sharing tactics with her team.

Zahide was an agile swimmer. "I'm a Sohni," she'd say and then tell the legendary tale of Sohni, of the river and beyond. She rescued me from the water with that same confidence and cool. Like a strong-willed guru, she had led the rescue, which was smooth and calm unlike the panicked attempts made by a fit senior student to pull me from the water, and she'd instantly won the respect of everyone at the pool.

I vaguely remember what happened afterwards. Zahide was wiping

---

1. According to the Qur'an, both the earth and the heavens, which consist of a solid sphere surrounding the earth, are made up of seven layers each.

the beads of water off my forehead with one hand and pushing my head back by pressing against my chin with her other. My eyes had probably been fixed on the distant wooden ceiling of the pool, which was grey and looked like moonlight. At the same time, I felt the presence of a shadow pierced intermittently by light. In the ripples of that shadow, I felt my body adjusting to life once again as my chest heaved like a pair of bellows, but I was unable to speak.

"It's all over," Zahide said, "don't be afraid."

After the shadow began to slowly fade away, I realized that it was actually a crowd of foolish students who, like us, had nothing better to do than to swim at that hour.

I was wet and my back ached, but I felt like I was on the verge of breaking into laughter.

"Go on, laugh," Zahide said. Years later, when they pulled me out of the rubble after that massive earthquake, I laughed just like that, after being buried under the rubble for thirty-six hours. I could barely make out the light streaming down and the shadows were like a glowing flicker rising from the pool up towards the ceiling; it hurt, but I started laughing, loudly and without fear.

"Laugh," she said. "You're right, this is life and there's nothing else we can do but laugh."

In my twenties, it was with Zahide that I had my first taste of laughter in the face of life. Even when she was feeling quite down, she would still insist that every moment in life is a miracle. Her graduation date was drawing near. We both knew that there were advantages to working as a dentist in a country like the United States. The dentistry diploma she'd received in Pakistan was worthless outside the country, so she'd had to start again from the very beginning. One time she confessed, "Deep down, I've never felt so humiliated in my life." She said she felt like that because she was from Pakistan, where extremist Islam

constantly threatened to boil over. Still, being a Muslim was important for Zahide. One day, she planned on moving back to Kashmir,
to the valley so dear to her father, so she could serve her own people.
She was an idealist, like many people from the third-world who want
to keep the ground beneath their feet from slipping away.

That was one of our common dreams: going back to our home
countries. And not long after we met, Zahide did go back. She got
married, but her idealism stirred her to desire more, so she returned
to the United States. It was as though that were a thousand years
before, as if a huge hole had been rent in the fabric of time.

If the Zahide of that day was the one in that article written by Jan
Gabriel, who was yesterday's Zahide? Who does that laughter belong
to? After I'd started laughing that night by the pool, she'd chuckled
at first, and her laughter rose into a crescendo, crystallizing and hanging in the air. Whose laughter was that? Does the past truly have the
power to mock us like that?

As I mulled over that article, I recalled her cheerful laughter. Life
sometimes plays with such ordinary moments and the ordinary feelings
they inspire. And then you're left dumbstruck. At the time, hearing
her laughter echo through my memory made me feel as though I were
short of breath; but then that inability to grasp reality was immediately
followed by a deluge of possibilities that I've never been able to completely reject. That was me, unable to know reality, but understanding
it in that way.

As I sat there lost in thought, I felt a hand touch my shoulder.

I jumped in my chair.

It was Nadir. After gazing at me intently for a few moments, he
said, "What's the matter, Emel? You look like you've seen a ghost.
You're white as a sheet."

"I think I may have seen a ghost," I said.

5

Nadir's sister Leyla, who was a real estate agent, picked us up just outside campus and drove us downtown. For some time now she'd been living in Maryland with her second husband. Getting the scholarship had been good for Nadir, and he was glad that he could be closer to where his sister lived after all those years apart. Two days before, as we smoked during the break in our class on New Conservatives, I'd said, "My biggest problem in this city is that I can't find a place to stay." He told me not to worry, that his sister would help me find a place. And he was right. A client of hers from Azerbaijan was apparently renting out the ground floor apartment of his house in the middle of town. The rent wasn't cheap by any means, but the Pont Foundation would cover half of the rent and I could pay the rest with my personal allowance for the time being.

By the time we arrived at the house, the snowfall had whipped into a blizzard, and we rushed inside. Wet as snowballs, we were met by a golden retriever whose red collar identified him as "Stray" and a woman whom I guessed to from Moldova. Stray, a big off-white ball of fur, rubbed against all of us one by one. The Moldovan woman said he was tame as could be and always did that when they had guests. There as a sofa by the entryway, and we sat down without even taking off our coats. Before we arrived, Leyla had mentioned that the house was built in the eighteenth-century and had been renovated about four years before. But rather than smelling of renovations, the house was filled with the cloying smell of dust. I'd never seen such a dusty house. Everything was covered in a film of grime, which seemed to be the primordial element infusing the space: the rugs, couches, large television, DVDs lying around, mug on the coffee table, framed picture of a ship caught in a storm hanging on the wall, the clock which was surrounded by a fan of spring twigs . . . Even the yellow walls seemed to be dusty, and the glass top of the coffee table was caked in an opaque layer of dust. The snow melting on our boots turned into sludge on the carpet, as did the water dripping from our coats when we sat on the leather sofa.

I think the dust was the reason that the three of us refused when the Moldovan woman asked if we'd like to have something to drink. We just sat there, wondering if we would melt and mix in with the sludge.

The Moldovan woman left the room, and we were left alone with Stray. He was a ball of energy, rolling on the floor, jumping into our laps and gnawing at the carpet. When the clock struck four and a bird emerged, singing like a cross between a budgerigar and a quail, Stray went crazy. As he leaped again and again up the wall trying to reach the clock, we heard someone call out, "That's enough, Stray." We turned and saw a man descending the stairs like the prince of darkness, swathed in black, exuding mystery. Ali, my new landlord.

He flashed us a smile of gold teeth.

Leyla was the first to speak. She told him that I was from Turkey and that I'd be staying in DC on a scholarship from Pont, which she said was a prestigious journalism grant offered jointly with Georgetown University, and she mentioned that I was the chief editor of foreign news at a top newspaper in Istanbul. As she went on and on about me,

I listened with my mouth agape; was I really all that? She promised to find a new tenant after I left, and suggested that if Nadir could extend his stay, perhaps he could rent the place. She added that I was her friend as well, and said that I'd pay two months' rent in advance— since we'd discussed that in the car, she looked at me at that moment and I nodded approvingly, and she went on to say that, as the landlord, Ali would benefit as well, due to the fact that I would host parties and invite Ali and his family too, so as an Azerbaijani businessman, he would have the chance to meet journalists from all around the world. Then she paused and took a deep breath.

"Well, that sounds just fine," Ali said. His hair was plastered back, glistening with hair gel, jet-black and hard. "Leyla, if you say that it's okay, then it's fine with me too," he added. Then he turned to me and said, "Turks and journalists are more than welcome in my place. You can move in right away. But first, Emel, you might want to see where you're going to live."

Nadir and I glanced at each other.

Nadir approved with a warm smile.

I spoke up for the first time.

"Ali, Leyla mentioned that the flat has some furniture. May I ask what there is?"

"If you decide to rent the place," Ali said, "you'll have everything you'll need. You could even move in tonight. My wife Nigar can give you a blanket and a comforter."

"That would be wonderful," I said.

Leyla, who had talked herself out of breath just a minute ago, cut in: "By the way, where is Nigar and your daughter?"

"They went to visit their aunt. They should be back soon," he said.

Leyla said, "Please send them my regards," and stood up, brushing off the remaining drops of water from the snowflakes melting on her cashmere coat. We followed suit and stood up as well.

Stray continued playing and running about, but he was far more subdued than that during energetic performance he'd put on before Ali made his entrance. As we were walking out the door, he howled plaintively.

From the outside, the ground-floor apartment looked like an extension of the house that had been squeezed under the staircase. Once we were inside, that perception intensified. The ceiling was low, at least two feet lower than normal. And the flat seemed to be the source of all the dust in the house. The smell of cheap wood pervaded the flat, which had the small windows typical of homes in DC, and there was a few feet of space outside each one. But you couldn't even enjoy the small, unkempt garden out front because none of the windows faced it. Apparently the only reason why it was called a garden-floor apartment was the fact that it was on the same level as the garden. For the first time since we arrived I pondered over the rent: "Am I going to pay $1,500 for this prison cell?" The ceilings of the two small rooms in the back were even lower, and they sloped down in a way reminiscent of Stray's doghouse so that you couldn't even stand up straight. The only reason you'd go into the bedroom with its double bed would be to sleep. There wasn't even enough room for a nightstand, so you couldn't even enjoy having a bedside lamp. In the second room, which was more like a storage room, there was a wardrobe that was so big it left little room for anything else; it would have been more appropriate to call it a wardrobe room than a bedroom. For the first time in DC, I felt tall, which is strange for someone like me who is just over five feet tall. The space that Ali called the living room was no bigger than a hundred square feet and it opened onto the adjoining kitchen which had a square table in the middle. Pointing to the coffee maker and the toaster on the kitchen counter, Ali said,

"You're welcome to use these as well."

If I were claustrophobic, there was no way I could have lived in that place. In all honesty, the only reason I was able to bear the tightness of the flat was the treatment I'd undergone after my experience in the earthquake. Nonetheless, I desperately wanted to get out of the heat and stuffiness of the flat. But if I didn't rent it, I wondered, where would I stay during the months that remained? I recalled that Leyla had mentioned that I could throw parties there. Sure that was possible, but only on one condition: no one much taller than me could be invited.

The flat obviously hadn't been built with Americans in mind. I thought of Richard Shelton from the *Washington Post*; standing at six feet two and probably weighing around 220 pounds, how would he ever fit? Enjoying the irony, I thought to myself, "It would be just perfect for him!"

As we were going out, I turned to Nadir and said, "This place would be just perfect for Richard Shelton." Unable to resist, at the same time we both said, tongue-in-cheek, "You don't say!"

Outside, the night was illuminated by the whiteness of the road. The grey gloom of the weather had ushered in dusk early, and the elegance of the street was accentuated by the warmth of the nearby cafés and bars. Leyla spoke up: "We'll take it."

Like a rushing snow plow, Leyla slipped past Ali with his gelled hair and, seeing the hesitation in my expression, said, "Dupont Circle's right over there. Don't let this place get away!" We got in the car and, on Leyla's insistence, went to an Italian pizza place in Friendship Heights near the campus. That was one of her favorite places. Her neighbor's cousin worked there, so she always got special treatment. Despite the cold weather, the restaurant was fairly busy, but Leyla managed to get us one of the best tables in the restaurant. The topic of discussion that night after having visited my new flat, which Leyla constantly referred to as being "right next to" Dupont Circle, was the small places where we've lived, and the conversation turned to Nadir and Leyla's past and childhood memories. But it was the discussion about Richard Shelton that was most surprising of all.

When I mentioned his name, Leyla asked, "Richard Shelton? The Richard from the *Wash Post*?" And she quickly added, "No way, he's my neighbor. He's a prick if I've ever known one. All the stiffs in town know him." It turned out that she'd been helping Richard and his sister Shaena renovate their home. And she was right about him knowing the deceased. Richard had a page in *Metro*, the weekend supplement of the *Post*, which included sentimental obituaries of people who passed away that week, along with their pictures. Sometimes the obituaries were written in the first person and sometimes in the third person, and you could never tell if Richard had written them or if they were penned by the relatives of the deceased. Occasionally there was a column on the left side of the page which was about interviews that Richard conducted with people who hadn't died yet but soon would. In Leyla's words, that column "just went too far."

"I've never really looked carefully at his column. Do you know why he even got involved with something like that?" I asked.

"Frankly, Richard doesn't say much about it. But it's true, why would a journalist do such a page? I'm sure he has his own reasons. People say that he has some other talents as well. I'm not kidding! Once he even blurted something like, 'I can read people's minds!'" As she talked, she tried to wind up the strings of cheese dripping with sauce stretching from her fork to the mushroom pizza.

"Like a sixth sense?"

"If you ask me," Leyla said, "Richard is so inept that he can't even hammer a nail into a wall, but that's something else." She said "inept" again, pursing her lips, and then burst into laughter. That's actually how Richard talked, with pursed lips, his voice hoarse as if a hose had been jammed down his throat.

Nadir burst out laughing as well, and said, "Ten years may have gone by, but my sister is still the same bubbly young girl."

He was right. Leyla had a timeless genuineness and exuded an energy that was simply riveting. I felt as though I were sharing a moment that was a celebration of something, a special moment that bore traces of the past, with two close friends, not two people I hardly even knew. When I tried to express this, and failed miserably in the process, Leyla said kindly, "There's no need to force yourself to say anything." That was just like the moment I was unable to express; in fact, I didn't really have the desire to say anything at all. All I had was my present situation: a scholarship, an empty house where I could sleep at night, Richard Shelton's seminar tomorrow, interviews for which I had to make appointments, and the gratitude I felt for this brother and sister from Iran.

All the same, I made a rather strange comment. Perhaps the wine had gone to my head: "Telling things is the plague of the times."

Just then, Leyla's neighbor's cousin approached our table and asked through his prominent front teeth, "Is everything okay with your dinner?" The oddness of the statement I'd made drifted off into the soft light and glowing atmosphere of the restaurant, vanishing into of its depths.

Although Nadir and Leyla insisted, I didn't go to Leyla's place that night. I felt a strange wind blowing, not just outside but within me as well. As I got on the subway, I knew where to go: Union Station. When first I arrived in DC, that was where the shuttle from Dulles Airport dropped me off; or perhaps I should say that it abandoned me there, leaving me all alone. But there is something unique about stations; if you ever find yourself at a point in your life when you want your luck to change, or if you feel like you need to turn back time, they are the best place to go. When I finally got to the station it was quite late and I had the feeling that if I went inside, the cold of winter would be put on hold, everything would be turned back. But I hesitated. Perhaps it would be better to get in a taxi and find a place to sleep on campus? No, everything had changed. I had the key to a flat of my own, even if it did share certain characteristics with a doghouse. But I shouldn't be unfair; compared to the room I'd had to share with a Syrian colleague for the last two weeks, that ground-floor apartment belonging to Ali and his enigmatic family was like a royal suite. Although it may have resembled a bell jar, when I opened the door, it would fill with fresh air. I liked the idea of having a place just for myself. I could come and go as I pleased, and do what I wanted when I wanted. And for that reason I decided to go to station, despite the late hour.

With my grey coat and my suitcase, I glided through the revolving door into that station that whispered of American winters. Earlier that afternoon I'd put my suitcase in the trunk of Leyla's car with the hopes that I would have a place of my own.

Although I was hardly aware of it at the moment, I knew deep down that all stations tend to look alike. An odd sensation passed through me; most probably just the heat of the past. I was used to that. Over time, all places start looking the same.

The revolving door carried me inside.

The high ceiling seemed to block everything out, creating its own time. I took in the surroundings, thinking that there was something fortress-like about the place: the café, ticket seller, ticket vending machine, glassy-eyed passengers, massive climbing ivy, echoing announcements. There, people were connected in other vast cities. It was a fortress that didn't defend itself against the outside; the best defense was to let itself out. Just like that first night when I arrived in the city, I walked all the way to the platform where the trains to New York departed and sank into the blue imitation leather seats in the waiting room. That was the space that brought together the rails, passengers, and journeys. As they sat there reading newspapers and eating snacks, the other passengers somehow all seemed alike, and that's why the thought occurred to me that all journeys arrive at the same destination.

On the seat to my right, a woman was beginning to doze off. As her head fell forward, she would almost wake up, but then her body, accustomed as it was to the pull of gravity, continued pulling her back to sleep. I noticed that there was a copy of last weekend's issue of *Metro*, the supplement to the *Washington Post*, on the metal coffee table between us. My head cleared at once. We'd just spent all night talking about Richard, and there was his column. How strange life can be! Somehow my feet had carried me through the night to that station, only to bring me face to face with Richard Shelton's page. The woman next to me had fallen into a deep sleep, snoring with a rhythmic whistle that said everything was normal. I began to read, keeping time with her rhythm.

Richard was one of my seminar instructors; in the introductory class, he'd introduced himself as a journalist working part-time for the *Washington Post* and said that he would be meeting with us once every two weeks in a seminar on journalism and human relations. We met several times after my arrival. His schedule kept him busy with teaching and helping scholarship students, and he always seemed to be rushing about on campus. Nadir had mentioned that Richard was actually one of the founders of Pont. Aside from what Leyla said, could it be a coincidence that his column was one of the most popular and received the most number of letters from readers? There were a number of black and white pictures of people, young and old, on the rather large page. The people were smiling in the close-up pictures and beneath them were the dates of their births and deaths. All of them had passed away, some a few days before, others in the past few weeks. There were people wearing evening gowns and others in uniforms. There was a picture of a person with their cat, and in another, someone was leaning against a tree in a garden. Some of the people looked out of the photographs with an expression of deep sadness, while others' eyes gleamed with happiness. The section that Leyla had mentioned was not in that issue. In the lower right corner, however, there was another section that caught my eye. It was dedicated to birthdays. Richard had seemingly randomly selected people from the pages of history who were born on that day but were no longer living. Despite the fact that they were no longer among the living, their birthdays continued to be celebrated. Sometimes the simplest of statements can transport you to places beyond your imagination; the words "happy birthday" were having precisely that effect on me. On the page before me there were pictures of several people, and they were all dead, gone from the world. I didn't even want to think about where those two words could be trying to take me. Beyond the limits of sanity? Very likely so. And the explicitness of it all, the utter lack of discretion, was simply too much for me. The boldness of those lines was enough to open the gates of my memory. They held no secrets. Death holds no secrets. Just like those days in my life when everything was out in the open. I'd managed to shake it all off. The sense of nakedness I'd felt was the heaviest price I'd had to pay for the past, but I'd succeeded in getting over it.

How? By forgetting. I forgot about the corpses, driving from my mind the fact that they had once been living people.

You get off at that stop called insanity, madness, delirium. Injections, days and days of therapy, meeting one on one, gathering in groups. You wait for your pain to exhaust its allotted time in your body and soul. And in the end, everything grows old, together with your tears, memories, toyshops, maternity wards, obstetricians, your womb, cough syrups, pajamas, hugs, suckling, baby bottles. Everything wears thin. Until you wake up one morning and there is the smell of bread toasting at a neighbor's home. You want to wake up and smell bread. You want the smell of bread to permeate your body, from under your nails to the very tip of your nose, even your bellybutton, mind, and hair. Bread is life, and that is what you want. You want to see that life goes on, you want to get better. That's why you want to go the graves of your son and husband. The dead don't live; you now want to know that. In the most selfish way you want that. So that you can move on, you want to believe that the dead are dead and that they have no connection with the world. Believing?

That's what guides you. Not believing threatens your very being. You don't want to know the reasons behind creation, the simple truths drifting among the realities of life discovered by alchemists. You don't want the meaning underlying those truths to be laid bare. In short, you don't want to draw God's wrath, because there are things that should not be left in the open.

Richard Shelton's lines before me seemed to be trying to do just that. It was like a damnation of humanity.

The dead should not be among the living. I had to put an end to it.

Abruptly I stood up, waking up the woman next to me who was snoring with flourishes of whistles. "What happened?" she said, taking a deep breath. We both had the same worried look in our eyes: that uneasy look of being woken up! Trying to explain my desperation, I made an inexplicable gesture, but gave up and simply apologized. Of course, she didn't understand what I was trying to say, and merely shook her head dismissively and then she turned away from me, settling into her seat to go back to sleep.

I, on the other hand, knew I had to leave there at once with my suitcase and the *Metro* supplement. I walked as fast as I could as I pulled my suitcase towards the main hall among the passengers going the other way on their way to New York.

Everything should be put in the past and stay there. Even that moment. Otherwise, I couldn't live. Otherwise, I couldn't breathe.

Moving along at the same clip, I entered the revolving door. And I spun.

Just like in the movies.

With that turn, my reason left me, vanishing into the distance. My reason fled, not heeding the boundaries of lives, not heeding those yet to be drawn, always meant to be drawn, and left in its place my feelings.

Outside.

I was outside again, but it wasn't cold. An intense heat seared my body. From that moment onward, all stations seemed to merge into one. Time spun back and I tumbled into the cavernous depths of my memories. The door in which I whirled around with my suitcase and gray overcoat must have taken me, young and full of enthusiasm, to Istanbul's Haydarpaşa Station, and I was wearing a red and orange summer dress. My heart was full of joy.

That's what must have happened.

I must have been coming from Adapazarı, from my mother's place, to Istanbul. Who's that? There was a boy next to me. I was holding his hand. He was yelling, "Mom, I need to pee!" "Wait," I was saying, "just wait a little, we're almost there." We were coming down the steps, feeling the heat of the sun.

At that point I would get confused. My heart would say, "You've never been to Adapazarı, you're wrong," but my mind would say, "You went from Istanbul to Adapazarı. You were wearing that dress. You went alone. Your son was in Adapazarı at the time. Your sister had a wedding the next day, and her henna party was happening that night. That's why you were going from Istanbul to Adapazarı. You were full of joy." I can never be sure. I remember some parts roughly, details skipped over as if they were memorized scenes from a life I'd lived for someone else. Other memories were so scored into my mind that they could have happened yesterday.

I was going up the stairs backwards, like a movie played in reverse.

The station was playing a trick on me and my mind.

Wearing that red and orange dress, I looked through the huge entrance of Haydarpaşa Station and saw an August day in Istanbul. I went down the stairs, towards the seashore. "Where is he?" I was asking. Who was I asking about?

Selim. I've been waiting for Selim. Selim is stuck in traffic again, he can't come. When is he ever on time anyway? But even this can't disturb my joy. It's been unbelievably hot the last few days. The mist over the sea was like a hazy smoke screen. You can't call it mist anymore; it's a curtain hiding the truth, uncompromising, and it doesn't seem it will ever lift. You can't bear to look at it; it pulls you into its depths and won't let go.

I have to make it to Naz's henna party. We can't afford to miss this train, Selim. Besides, you know that tomorrow is my birthday. We'll celebrate both at the same time. That's what Naz said: "Your birthday would pass unnoticed at the wedding, Abla. It doesn't matter whether we do it on the 16th or the 17th of August. So let's celebrate your birthday at my henna party."

The red and the orange dance in the heat. I'm waiting. I'm waiting for the attack to hit me and then blow past. Selim doesn't show up, he's late again. He can take the later train. I have to go. And in any case trains are for friendships, not for tired marriages.

"Excuse me," someone calls out, "do you need a taxi?"

The heat vanishes, along with the summer day. Bitter cold air whips across my face. I am immersed in a true America of my own making.

"No," I reply. I wait, breathing in and out. Finally, steam that had crystallized in the cold air rises up within me. No, I'm not waiting for a taxi!

I am nothing more than a living corpse.

A dead person living in her own hell.

During our third interview, Zahide told me about how she was put in the rendition program after she was released from the hospital and described what she went through after arriving in New York. As she said, it was a road to hell. In that interview she placed special emphasis on numbers and details. She gathered her untidy memories together with the documents and dates I'd obtained through my research and took notes, one by one, in her memory, which had become like that of a schizophrenic, as if drawing a genealogy of her own life.

In the beginning, she was quite confused. She wasn't even sure if the plane had taken off from Dulles. "Since we flew to New York," she'd say, "they must've flown me out of Reagan, where they have domestic flights." I believed that for a while, but there were some inconsistencies. Then I obtained some information from journalists and researchers conducting research on the subject. There was no such rendition flight out of Reagan to New York. There were a few flights, but they went to New Jersey's Teterboro Airport, and the crew would change planes there. With those flights, there was no detention, just direct rendition. Zahide's Phoenix, however, flew directly from North Carolina, the central headquarters, to Dulles, and from

Dulles to Teterboro and then they went to New York by car. After a brief period of detention in New York, she was sent to Sweden with the same plane and crew, and from there to Amman. Phoenix, the Simurgh, stayed at the Swedish airport for three or four hours and then continued its journey after a couple of Muslims arrested on Swedish soil were brought to the plane.

You were right, Zahide said. It's simply confusion, what can you do. That trip of mine was the journey of the Simurgh to Mount Qaf.[2] You were right, but that changes nothing now.

Levent Bey, in light of the information you provided, it seems that a plane took off from North Carolina on December 2, 2001, at 7 a.m. local time. Not long after, around forty-five minutes, the plane landed at Dulles Airport in Washington, DC. It was a sleek and stylish bird. After refueling, it was time for the passenger to appear. The passenger—Pakistan-born American citizen Zahide Sohni Mühür, myself actually, blindfolded, shackles on my feet, hands bound behind my back—was taken from the waiting room and put on the plane. Based on the information you gave, the plane was a Phoenix; the Simurgh appeared to belong to a legitimate American company registered with the IRS, but actually it was a private plane chartered by the CIA. It was a Phoenix IV jet. Wasn't it?

Here I confirm what she said. Then she tells me, with no particular emphasis, what she has on her mind.

The male and female voices of the masked agents wearing Timberland boots and dressed in black sounded sincere. Still, that was the beginning of the end, she'd sensed it. Then Zahide Sohni Mühür knew the past was history and the future was but a promise. It

---

2. Mount Qaf is an emerald mountain that, according to Islamic legend, was at the farthest point of the earth, the boundary between the realm of humans and the realm of the spirits. In the legend, the Simurgh, the bird-king of all flying beasts, lived on Mount Qaf.

was only the present that concerned her, and that was the first time it felt so close.

She hoped they would take her blindfold off at least after she was put on the plane. She had come all the way from the hospital like that, blindfolded. Karen had said that they would be taken off after a while, both the blindfold and the chains on her wrists. That's what she'd said, in Urdu. But what would it change? Did it matter if passengers with different fates happened to share a common language? The whiteness of Karen's bones brushed against her dark hands. Another injection? Yes. Of course, yes. For some reason Karen's hands were icy cold. Her voice, however, was warm, soft. She was talking to Zahide about her own children. Did she know that Zahide's children were dead? That Zahide was the only one who had survived that horrendous shock? She knew. Of course she knew.

Zahide would have more than enough time to think about what her crime was. Karen knew that as well. Or perhaps during the torture, she'd just die. Karen also knew that. That was the best way.

It was time for Zahide to get ready for a journey of unknown duration. She had the bearing of a bad actor trying to warm up for a role in which she knew she would forget her lines. But she was ready. For the accusations, for the signing of blank documents. Ready. In any case, she didn't have a soul. Her body, on the other hand, was ready for everything. Karen knew that, too.

When her blindfold was taken off, Zahide saw that she was in a luxury twelve-seat jet. She identified the Timberland boots with a strange sense of priority. Then she noticed the seats. They were brown leather seats, the color of milky coffee.

Such a color, she had never imagined it existed.

A dance on the leather seats. Zahide was now ready for that dance after the injection Karen had given her in her left arm. Ready to tell the story she was expected to tell. But there must be no break in between.

We're going to take a picture of you, Zahide.

Let them.

Zahide would look at the camera with sealed mouth and eyes. She'd murmur, I'm ready to go the land of the dead.

Then she would hear that sound. It was the sound of the land of the dead. She insistently repeated that: the land of the dead. The sound of the land of the dead. It was a familiar sound . . .

Who?

You are now ready to cross a magical threshold, Zahide.

Who who who?

You need to know this means crossing over to the zone of rebirth.

Who was she?

You're a true hero now. Only a hero can take the risk of getting lost in the unknown. And there is only one condition: you must play dead. On this trip we'll be taking you to the womb of the world, but don't let the gatekeepers waiting at the threshold deter you.

Who?

Most of this is to protect the real temple of the world from fake heroes, to intimidate them. Time will come to an end. Be prepared for that. On this journey taken by your spirit, you'll be subjected to a true test, and if you're brave enough, you'll find what you're looking for. That's why fiery dragons, roaring lions, lurking snakes and growling bulls with outspread wings shouldn't scare you. Heaven on earth is yours when you overcome fear.

Who, who?

And if you have the ability to cross that threshold, the promise of heaven will be yours. The notion of God might frighten you in the beginning, because we're used to being wary. But the fact is, the inability to comprehend God means seeing Him as the devil and avoiding

Him. The fact is, God exists when He's not avoided, because real fear is hidden away in unworldly enlightenment. If you're enlightened, you can no longer inflict harm, not on yourself nor on others. Darkness, on the other hand, is malice; it's hell on earth. That's where people feel comfortable and levelheaded. Far from God and truth, they're comfortable, casual and bigoted. The journey to the land of the dead is a step towards putting life at the center and reaching eternity. Coming into being again. But for this, Zahide, you must first take the risk of being destroyed.

Fine, but who?

Who? Who knows.

Some close, some far away. Your mother, father, neighbors, husband, relatives, roads, acquaintances, complete strangers . . .

A woman with no one.

Zahide-Sohni-Sohni will not remember that time.

Sohni is fast asleep. Everyone follows their own path.

For this, Zahide, you must first take the risk of being destroyed. In order to see your dead and meet them, you must relax, Zahide.

RICHARD. It was Richard.

Richard's voice was the sound of the land of the dead.

It was the voice of Richard that said, "Everything happens for a reason, don't ever forget that." That was the Richard who was occasionally kind.

"Try to relax, Sohni," Karen would say. "We're going to fly to New York."

"No," said Zahide. "To the land of the dead . . ."

She closed her eyes. Richard's image was right there beside her. The old one from Kensington, Maryland. The house. So close.

I had no fear of dreams or apparitions, and even though it was quite far, I decided to walk home from the station. But after passing by a few stops, I got on the subway again. Holding the key that Leyla had slipped into my hand at dinner, I waited for my inner tumult to die down. Sometimes the smallest sign can give you the courage you seek. Since I was going to live there, I had to get used to Ali's ground floor apartment. I knew how to open the doors of lonely homes, how to plunge into their scent of loneliness. The rest was just a matter of getting used to it.

The late afternoon snow had been relentless, and the small garden near the entrance of my new home had filled up with snow. I looked at the upper floors; the lights of the living room were still on and I heard Stray bark. Other than that, it was rather quiet.

I thought briefly about continuing on my way as if there was nothing there for me.

I opened the door. It was stuffy inside, and there was that pervasive smell of dust. I hesitated. At that moment, I was overcome by a strange a fit of coughing. But it brought me to my senses.

There was no room for hesitation.

Where did I stand in relation to time? Even though I'd asked myself that question countless times, I thought it through clearly for the first time; in fact, I didn't stand anywhere in time, yet it always held me in its clutches. Having been trapped under rubble for thirty-six hours, I knew quite well the sway that time had over my body and soul.

No, it all was for that moment. To be able to say that everything was normal, that I could manage. I knew I couldn't make a clear choice between my past and present, no matter how much I may have wanted that, just as I was blinded to the light after having been buried all those hours. For weeks my eyes couldn't get used to the light of day; I was in a bottomless pit, but through my body I could tell if it was day or night. Later during those sessions of therapy in which my soul was mended, a psychiatrist whose name I can't remember told me that I perceived day and night through my body's knowledge. He also leaned in and whispered that, from then on, I could manage with the help of the codes in my body. I have no idea why he whispered that to me; perhaps it was a figment of my imagination, although I had to admit that he was right about the body and what it knows. A year after the incident, I began to question my body about my choices. Emotional choices took a heavy toll on me. The idea of adopting a child? The next day, my body would respond to the question. I'd wake up with a sore back, unable to get out of bed. Shrug everything off and go on a vacation? A migraine attack, lasting for a week. Naturally I asked myself even more terrifying questions as well. The thought of suicide was foremost among them. And of course it was absurd to ask such a question, but I was a mere captive of the questions that swirled in my mind. The question of death made my body turn rigid. I was out of breath, lifeless, and it was exactly at that point that I felt I had to make a choice between life and death.

I didn't need to be very optimistic. The answer "no" meant choosing to get lost in the lack of promises of an empty house rather than in the streets on a snowy night. And what I understood of the word "promise" entailed letting go of myself in the moment.

I sat down, slumping at the small kitchen table. I put the *Metro* with Richard's column on the table, turning to his column; all those cheerful faces of the dead. I couldn't read single a line. I drifted off to sleep.

It must have been long after midnight when I woke up to the sound of something rattling. It sounded as if someone was tapping on my table.

"They're here," I thought. Jumping up, I said out loud, "Richard's people are here." My own voice brought me back to life. I was alive.

And the dead were still on the table, looking up at me with their smiling faces. The energetic tapping was coming through the thin brickwork ceiling. In the depth of my sleep, I realized that it was the pattering of an animal's paws echoing down from above. Stray was saluting the small hours of night.

Many nights in my new home would be spent like that. As I slumped over the table under the weight of the events of the day, Stray moved about restlessly upstairs, jumping and leaping. Stray never slept at night. Despite what I told people, I didn't actually sleep in the strictest sense either. After all is said and done, I was also a Stray. Nor did I always sleep in bed. As he ran around, more dust would rain down on me from the ceiling. My nose grew rather accustomed to the smell of dust again, after all those years. In a state between sleep and wakefulness, I'd see every particle of dust cascading down like glitter. All night long the glitter fell as Stray ran around, filling me up to the pupils of my eyes with that gleam and glimmer.

Ever so slowly it drifted down. Stray. Sometimes I'd fall asleep down there, and sometimes I'd dance. There were articles that that I had to write, publications I had to read. The dust, the glitter, cascaded down over everything, flitting through my hair, muttering nonsense, but I was completely indifferent. Stray was a ball of energy, a live wire. Flakes of varnish, dust and dirt, fell nonstop covering everything, even behind the door, cascading down onto the refrigerator, onto my feta cheese, onto my jams, pickles, meat and liver. Shabby and forlorn, I was a glittery mess.

That was me.

That was the summary of me in the house.

I was a stray but I had an owner. That was to be my situation at home in the future. I liked it. I still like it.

As Stray clattered about upstairs, sometimes I would bray in my home below. We'd break the sound barrier and then speed faster than light. Every part of me was ablaze, gleaming. Anyone who saw me would think I was mad, but the real crazy one was Stray.

Actually all strays are raving mad. At least down there, among the foundations of the house. Emel was like that, Stray was like that.

Along with those adornments, lies fell upon me as well. Particle by particle, grains of dust. All strays know their fate and are defeated by fate.

He'd run around upstairs and I'd run around downstairs. In the middle of the night. Sometimes I'd drink a Bloody Mary, sometimes cheap champagne. I brushed aside what they'd told me: Don't lose yourself. I'd repeat that to my patched up soul: Don't you dare let yourself be lost.

But it was futile.

It no longer worked. All because of that glitter. Always that Stray. All because of those fickle circumstances. But only at night. Like that. Only when you're Stray.

When you don't have to tell anyone anything. Only like that.

Stray and I, we're jowl to jowl, night after night, under the glitter.

He'd weep upstairs, and I, downstairs.

9

For Emel, the next day began with a difficult morning mired in snow.
The snow rushed inside as soon as she opened the door and so it continued, all the same flurry.

Richard also went to school accompanied by the snow. In that hall
with high ceilings and windows enveloped in white, his gaze drifted
around with a warmth tinged by arrogance, but never once did he
look Emel in the eyes. His glances even drifted outside the window
and lingered on the snow. Then Richard said:

"All children who grow up near the sea dream that they can walk
on water. I think it's the same with most of you here. But I grew up
inland, away from the water, so I dream of flying through the air
when it snows."

In that class of fifteen students, his statement caught everyone off
guard. Sometimes when emotions are unexpectedly revealed, they are
met with an enthusiastic response. When you encounter that in the
pages of a book, you aren't as affected, but when it happens in life, you
may find yourself completely stunned.

That's why the class lapsed for a moment into deep silence, each
person captivated by a different memory that fluttered in their minds.
And then with wry smiles, they tried to meet Richard's eyes.

The abstract line that Richard drew between himself and the class didn't just make a distinction between people from the coastlands and those who grew up inland; it went far beyond that. But no one seemed to mind that departure just then. Because of what he'd said, they found Richard to be sincere and trustworthy, and they began to hang on his every word.

Despite the fact that the topic of the seminar was journalism and human relations, the lectures kept turning back to the issue of the New Conservatives. From the first day they'd arrived, Emel and her classmates had repeated conversations about those conservatives whose ideas may seem dated but were new in terms of their philosophy and the meaning they spread throughout the world. Actually, even that sufficed to show just what the Pont scholarship was all about. Naturally, however, the students weren't aware of the underlying themes. Everything was very serious, orderly and punctual. The actual emphasis was on world power and hegemony, as one former CIA official who attended the seminar had once said. They were talking about a new world empire, emphasizing the inevitability of its existence. The emphasis was so subtle that no one noticed what lay beneath. It was frequently mentioned that everything in the world had gotten out of hand and that it was now necessary to take certain measures. And the global media was to play a large role in those efforts. It was argued that some local and national newspapers were still pursuing romantic democratic and liberal rights, but the matter had unfortunately reached a point that such sentimentality could no longer resolve the situation. No doubt there was a need for the world to be reshaped. But there was a strange expectation that people had to be wise in terms of understanding and supporting that power. Saying that "everything was getting out of hand" seemed to mean that people should just stand by as the world tumbled into the depths of hell. With its "magnificent" military, the United States was argued to be the only power capable of putting an end to that calamity. The world was at such a crossroads that only hi-tech weapons could usher in an age where dreams came true. And by that point, everything would be possible, even that which seemed to defy all logic. It was the means that differed. It was as if the entire community, including Richard, had obtained the world's magic words, and all that needed to be done was formulate the secret.

After talking about flying, Richard briefly touched upon the principle of flight espoused by the New Conservatives. The documentary film Richard Shelton had made, parts of which he was going to show towards the end of class, would be used to support his claims. According to Richard, conservatism had become so caught up in the world of business that in the previous five or ten years, politics had lost its power of imagination. And when that happens, he argued, life shudders to a halt. Even beyond that, however, the values which make people who they are become lost as well. "You see," Richard said, "when the doors of the Republicans were opened to the New Conservatives, a new wind blew through the world media, and rightfully so. It was like the intellectualism and imagination of the left, which the right had lacked until that point, had been welcomed in their midst!"

At that point, Richard seemed to have felt a need to talk about himself a little. Perhaps he wanted to deny that he was one of the New Conservatives. That intuition may have been right, because as he focused on the importance of imagination, he let it slip that he believed that the ideas of the left led people into deception; the liberal diction he employed to try to cover up his slip merged with the silence of the snow outside.

But Emel could no longer bear it. Speaking as the voice of the silent majority in the classroom, she asked in a rather girlish tone of voice:

"But could you get on to the point of what the real goal of the New Conservatives actually is?"

Richard stopped and looked at Emel. That's when he truly saw her. Not with the kind and forlorn looks of the towering figure who for days had been there at the front of the class, but rather like someone whose eyes momentarily flashed with malice. Just for a moment, nothing more. A second later he was the kind and forlorn Richard again, the man who is blind to Emel, the usual disconcerted, caring, warm Richard.

"Can you remind me what your name is?" he asked.

Then he launched into an explanation. Was he really explaining anything though? It was more like Richard had written her a letter, skipping over only the opening "Dear Emel" and begun reading it in a single breath.

Sometimes a lot of ground is covered in order to travel a very short distance; Richard knew that. And that's what made him who he was; anything he didn't know, on the other hand, was irrelevant anyway.

"Everything's important," began Richard. "The minutest details. Questions, their answers, silences, escapes, lies."

After a short pause he continued:

"Telling you that the left is wrong could be described as just a slip of my profession, which has been ingrained in my own personality. But believe me when I say that I'm referring to the distant past. I'm not sure how I can best explain this. Of course you can't expect me to explain such a secret in fifty-two minutes. There are some people who show the greatest ingratitude towards their lives, they forget about themselves. You see, I've never forgotten myself. Or maybe I should put it this way: Even if I don't quite confess that I'm one of those people, I most certainly do know what's what. People like that wait for a reason to reveal themselves, reasons they tend to ignore. I won't lie to you, I always waited for such reasons. The question you asked just now had such an effect on me. To give an example, when a friend of yours who you haven't seen in a long time comes and talks to you about the violation of rights in American foreign policy or the mole on your back, or asks you whether you still like vanilla ice cream, you answer with zeal. What triggers such a response is the questions, not the answers. The timing doesn't matter much, just for that reason. The questions are timeless. Your question is very open and universal. The New Conservatives are now a symbol of power in the world and their goal, put simply, is to take over the world. I think almost everything is hidden in that point. In power. But as I said, that and similar questions transcend time and place. Yet your answers seem to say that you're on top of everything, even though they're very subjective. Think of it like this: For years you haven't been able to stomach foreign policy one bit, the mole on your back isn't malignant melanoma, and in any case you haven't eaten vanilla ice cream in ages. And in fact, you don't actually care about any of it at all. Still, bolstered by answers, you're like a prophet spreading the light. You worship divine justice, you remember the day you felt your mole for the first time like it was yesterday, and you can feel deep down inside your revulsion for the smell of vanilla ice cream, which is like baby vomit. It's a pack of lies. Perhaps it wasn't like that before, maybe you weren't like that. You could have talked for hours about what responsibility meant for you and how you defined yourself."

Richard sighed deeply at that point and began gazing out the window again.

"Ah, those discussions. I had them myself. But when I saw that they came to nothing, I stopped. It means being insured, pure and simple. And that's no joke. I'm talking about your workplace, health insurance, severance pay, taxes you paid and will pay, and the hopes that these will offer you in return. I did all of that. But then I gave up, precisely because the answers didn't matter. Instead of discussing paradoxes, I thought about my payroll. I put my ideals into tangible form. The peace of mind afforded by being able to pay your mortgage, of knowing your annual income, was much more profound than every type of nihilism. I lost my faith in lonely men talking to toilet paper; I became bored with the generation of '68 because now there were NBA games. I was a fan of the Wizards, even though they kept losing. Our Magicians, you know. In brief, that was the extent of my belief in magic, to the extent that it suits a fifty-five-year-old white American male.

"There's no need to hide it, I'm a liberal. I know that could also become tedious after a while. As you might guess, I find the current administration extremely meaningless. I want our troops to return from Iraq, and I want our economy to recover as soon as possible.

"However, that doesn't mean going out on the streets to find a solution. Well, my friends, you know where the solution is?

"What I'm talking about is my comment which Emel, and Lord knows all of you, have misinterpreted. I believe conservatism will save the world. I'm pretty sure that the New Conservatives can pull that off. The idea of the right or of the reactionary thinking implicit in conservatism is the only hidden meaning that can save us from the doomsday into which the world is about to tumble. That was the reason for today's lapse, for all lapses made until today, brought about by those attempts to explore meaning explicitly. But it was a mistake, we were barking up the wrong tree. If you're not like those philosophers who withhold the secrets of life, if you believe that putting everything out in the open is the only solution, then you'll lose. I'd like to remind you of the words of Jesus: 'Give not that which is holy unto the dogs, neither cast ye your pearls before swine.' If that happens, as history has repeatedly shown, you can bet we'll be defeated. And we were defeated. What's meant by dogs and swine is the ordinary human mind. If you reveal all the strategies and secrets of life to the average person, they'll not only fail to understand them but will also turn around and tear you to pieces. That's what's happening in Afghanistan and the Middle East today. And we as a country went through this same agony during the Cold War. Vietnam was a total disgrace for us. Not because a lot of people died or because we lost the war. People die in wars, and losing is as natural as winning. No. Something else happened there. A policy that would drag our name through the mud for the next twenty years was formulated. A policy of confrontation and transparency. Thank God the rebels from those days are now candidates for Alzheimer's disease and museum exhibits, and we can breathe easy. What does the average citizen want? Not to be taken for an idiot. He wants to stand together proudly with his family, culture and flag, and boast about who he is. If what we're looking for is safety and moderation, here's a prescription for you. The United States and every other country in the world need such an approach. But if what we're looking for is chaos and being ashamed of who we are and what we've done, then take openness, democracy and transparency, and to hell with all of it. Secret tactics and strategies, secret services, have to be kept secret. Once such secrets become known, everything loses value. It's just like learning the secrets that God has kept from us since childhood. Knowing the secret of the elixir doesn't comfort us. On the contrary, it condemns us to the deepest of dungeons.

"My father was a soldier and scientist. He was actually more like a modern-day alchemist, and he had some pretty unusual ideas about the creation of the world. One day, he told me: 'Let me tell you the secret of Creation.' Of course, a small child can only infer one thing from that. Namely, that something that is already there will be recreated, and that is just what happened. My father had me conduct an experiment on the issue of creation. On a snowy day like today, he had me collect a jar of melted snow. For ten days, I kept the jar tightly closed. Then he told me to pour a third of this water into a clay pot at noon. And that's just what I did. Then I set the pot off in a corner. I can't remember how long I waited, but eventually my father told me it was time to get the pot. My father took a drop of his secret syrup—forgive my saying secret syrup, it was just fermented grape juice—and put it in the water. An incredible thing happened, something you may not believe. Strange fumes rose up from the liquid. Then my father put a couple more drops of the syrup into the water. And then something unbelievable happened. This time, light arose from the liquid. I was left dumbstruck. My father went on adding more drops: one drop every quarter of an hour, then two, three, then four, five drops, six . . . And I saw it. I saw something I wasn't supposed to see.

"Believe me, it was quite intense to witness something like that. It wasn't about God creating the world in six days. I actually saw how the world was created. It was indescribable. It was horrific, to be honest. It was too much, far too much.

"Truth is something like that.

"Politics, just like art, should not speak the truth. Revealing the truth doesn't just stir up the masses. No, it also leads them into chaos.

"That's why I believe in the New Conservatives. They could be lying, but what we really need are lies, not the truth.

"Do you know what that's actually like?

"I write for the *Washington Post*'s weekend supplement. Some of you may have seen my column. Commemorating birthdays doesn't bring those people back. That would be quite dangerous indeed. I'm not trying to argue that those people are alive when in fact they're quite dead. I'm not talking about ghosts here. No, nothing like ghosts at all. And please, don't think that I'm just trying to confuse you.

"Do you know what it's like? Think about war correspondents. No, I'm not a war correspondent. I don't want to be one. Being a war correspondent means that you have to state the facts as they are. I don't want to write about war. Especially these days. It's a very sensitive topic. And, you have to take sides. Either you're for it, or you're antiwar. I'm just a columnist who hands out lies. That's what I offer: a kind of paradise. To be honest, reporters terrify me. Real reporters are the philosophers of today. What they say hurts us, every single word. In that case, what should a columnist do? Drone on and on, surrounded by attractive pictures. And it's all for our own good. Columnists deserve every cent they get paid. They are the false prophets of our times. What more could we want? For that reason, I'd like to see you all become columnists in the future. Saving the world will be within your grasp. You'll develop such a clear understanding that you'll be able to convert all the poison in the world into power, and then make happiness arise from that power, which is in fact the holiness of the secret service and the sacredness of intelligence. That's precisely what the New Conservatives do. I can't go on without saying that you also have to be engaged in art, which is in such a state of exhaustion today. As you all know, art is in its death throes, for all the reasons I mentioned before. Art began falling apart the moment it began telling that which should remain untold. However, it is art that makes us human. Columnists carry much of the responsibility for seeing that art becomes a part of everyday life. It's a columnist's duty to meddle in everything. Painting, literature, philosophy, you name it. But that has to be done under the conditions I mentioned. You can use any style you want. You can swear, be vulgar, or be polite, but what you will do in the end is create a brand for yourself. It's all up to you. And there's more: You could also be a *true* writer, provided that you don't stray from the path I described. You can't reveal all the secrets of the world to an average person. Telling the truth just spells trouble. Not just today, though. It has for hundreds of years. Look at the snow outside. The instant you start thinking how each tiny snow-flake came into being, the trouble begins. Yet a snowy landscape is so relaxing to behold. There's a very clear distinction between the two. The first is an awareness of existence that would infuriate God and lead to modern nightmares. The second is a feeling of relaxation and comfort, a sense of security brought on by that."

Richard stopped for a moment to catch his breath. When he began speaking again, his tempo was even faster, keeping time with the blizzard that had begun raging outside. He began discussing third-world countries, arguing that Muslims constitute a risk group rather than a threat.

"If we want to talk about modern nightmares, the New Conser-vatives are actually creating illusions, every single one of them. We live in an age of risk, not an age of threats. Everything was easier for us during the Cold War. We had a single enemy. Yet now we're faced with an enemy with many heads. This is a risk that arises from Islam. Yes, it is a risk. Even if you know everything, you're still at risk. And in the end you get a society that feels insecure and you get insecure individuals. That's why I believe in the New Conservatives. They're not telling us the truth and they're doing a good job of it.

"What they're doing is right, if you get down to the bottom of it

"It may be hard to believe, but we need those lies to go on living. And of course there will be secret plans backing their cause. Nothing can be transparent. Transparency exists only in name, nothing more. When a secret becomes commonplace, it becomes ordinary, it is cheapened, and the balance in the world is upset. That's actually the essence of our religions as well. Don't get me wrong, I'm not arguing that New Conservatism is a religion, but the world cannot be saved by gibberish like transparency, equality, and fraternity. I really mean what I'm saying.

"Based on what I've told you, you may think I'm just a withdrawn pessimist, but I am not. I'm one of the most passionate journalists at my newspaper. There's no need to be modest about it. When you find your path, then you can truly run, even fly. But if you don't, there's no choice but to stand still, or even worse, plummet."

What Richard said after that seemed more reasonable. He talked about daily life, his fondness for basketball and football and the bamboo plants at his house, and then he showed a fifteen-minute documentary about the rendition program, which was described as one of the country's most "effective" plans of action to counter terrorism. After the film was over, I'm sure that four or five of the fifteen journalists who'd been invited on the Pont scholarship from the most troublesome regions of the world to that "land of new hope" toyed with the idea of inviting that white-haired, blue-eyed giant of a man to a rowdy snowball fight outside, the silhouette of the city shrouded in white rising up in the background. One of those journalists was Emel. She didn't know what dark thoughts the others may have harbored, but Emel had a burning desire to throw Richard into the snow and suffocate him in it. She was even more enraged when the film showed the faces of people deemed to be terrorists.

One of those pale figures was none other than Zahide Mühür. The face of the plague of our times . . .

If tracking down Zahide Mühür meant getting mixed up with Richard, that's precisely what Emel was going to do. First she thought of speaking with him. Her questions were obvious. Do you know Zahide? If so, how? When and where was that photograph taken? Do you know Jan Gabriel, the author of that article, the plague of our times? Do you have any documents which implicate Zahide as a terrorist? Emel knew well enough that that all the questions she'd ask would merely vanish in the blanket of white which had buried the sprawling campus grounds and began drifting towards the city. Whatever she asked, it seemed like the answers she'd get would only add to what she'd been told in class that afternoon and fizzle away. Although she knew it would probably prove fruitless, she still didn't give up on tracking Richard's shadow. They advanced slowly, Richard in front, she following behind. The scene would be etched in Emel's memory: snow piling up in drifts on the campus lawns, changing in places from white to grey, the whipping wind, the pale glow of the campus lights in the evening. The yellow light bathing the snow would falter with each step that Richard took, and more and more he'd start to resemble a shadow in search of its body, seeking out particles of light, a ghost rather than a living person.

10

Only her face is visible on the screen. She sniffles.

"I've been here for eighteen months," she says.

She looks to her right.

"I'm serving my sentence, whatever it is." She bows her head slightly.

"I've been treated very well here."

She pauses. She's staring blankly at the camera.

"I accept all the charges that have been brought against me."

She blinks, and then appears calmer. Her pupils are visibly dilated. She gulps a few times.

"I haven't been subjected to any inhuman treatment during those eighteen months."

There's a strange noise in the background.

"I was involved with the organization for four years. My job was to illegally move money for the organization."

She pauses again.

"I haven't been tortured."

She nods her head for no apparent reason.

"I'm from Pakistan. My ultimate dream was to cause damage all across the United States."

That was all. The only relationship I could establish with Zahide after all those years was through such admissions as I sat in a small reading-room in a library.

My intentions had changed completely, but now that I'd achieved what I'd set out to do, even gone farther than I'd hoped, I found myself able to do nothing but stand aghast.

My initial goal had been clear: to find out who Richard Shelton was. That was easier than I'd expected. When I pushed forward with a line of reasoning based on what, where, and how, I found the documentary quite easily, without having to decipher passwords or comb through special archives or confidential documents. I didn't even have to go to the campus library to find it. I came across the film at the small public library near my home, which shattered Richard's idea that "truth must never be injected in a blatantly obvious way into ordinary minds." On a Sunday afternoon, I watched the entire film, of which he had shown a small part in class; there were just four elderly men and myself in the reading room. The two-part DVD, entitled *The Rendition*, was in the documentary section, which apparently received few visitors. Considering the confessions of Zahide and the four other people introduced in the film, it seemed that the documentary shouldn't be titled *The Rendition* but rather something along the lines of *The Five Horsemen of the Apocalypse* or *The Five Musketeers*. How much more creative that would be! And, of course, there was another crucial point: almost everyone displayed the same reaction, including the senator who didn't want me to disclose his name in the article I planned to write about the program. Secrecy was clearly a top priority. Yet everything was so out in the open and accessible that even buying a concert ticket would be more complicated. And naturally, that led me to doubt myself at times, as I was doing at that very moment. But that Sunday afternoon, when a group of people had gathered downstairs in the library for a virtuosos meeting despite the snowy weather, I found out about the connection between Richard Shelton and Zahide. Occasionally I heard wisps of music drifting down from the gallery above, the sound of a violin being played by timorous hands. But it wasn't just the connection between Richard and Zahide that came to light; I also began to see that he had played a role in what happened to her, considering his connection with the three other people as well.

That realization infused the reading room, occupying my thoughts from midafternoon until it was time for the library to close.

The documentary was just like our day and age: secret yet obvious, hidden yet signifying nothing. Being aware of that, however, was no consolation. And naturally I couldn't say that the rendition program itself meant nothing. But that documentary film, a compilation of Richard's own footage and materials he compiled from elsewhere, was a big zero. It was the mere product of a mind's banal perspective on the statements of four people given under inhuman circumstances, forcing humor through those stories with uncanny prevarications— yes, such a drive was clearly evident in the work. While the country had sought out fantasy in different ways twenty years before, it was now explicitly trying to draw the army, military might and the national flag into its schemes; I could see that the underlying idea of the film was to provoke people through approval of that.

Watching the film from beginning to end was absolute torture. The initial excitement I had felt at having found Zahide, the feeling of victory that surged through me when I found the film, was torn to shreds in the face of that grotesque parody of a documentary. I felt utterly cheated. It hurt me to see that Richard could be so biased and macho, and I was devastated by the heavy-handed propaganda that existed between the lines. The fact that he had blatantly turned Zahide into an instrument for his own ends was simply shocking. Although he took shelter in the guise of arrogance, the ineptitude of his filmmaking couldn't be concealed. The film claimed to "closely investigate" the lives of Zahide and four other people who were deemed terrorists, but the shallowness of the framework was clear to see: a few experts were consulted, a couple of men and women who were Muslim were interviewed on the flimsy grounds of giving an "objective perspective," there were shots of minarets accompanied by the sound of calls to prayer, bizarre poems were read, and Latin quotations by Dante were used to reinforce the dramatic element. Those Muslim detainees, among whom Zahide was the only woman, were depicted as jackals of the age, or perhaps it would be better to say "plagues" of the age. I knew all four of them. Yusuf Rıza, or Yusuf the saxophone player, whose house Zahide and I stayed at during a trip to New York, Zahide's husband Dam and Zahide's brother Bilal. And occasionally there were scenes of Zahide's father, who had been killed some time in the past. He was referred to as the ringleader in the film, which was the ultimate absurdity. I had my doubts about Dam and Bilal, but it was inexplicable how Zahide and Yusuf had been implicated. There are times when you feel a sense of guilt weighing down on the nape of your neck. Guilt for people you didn't even murder, blood you didn't shed, a building you didn't destroy, a bomb you didn't detonate. I think there are times when we all feel that we are somehow guilty. And at that moment, that's what I felt. The documentary created such an ambiance, generating tension and a rush of other violent emotions that made you want to strangle the first Muslim you happened to encounter. The way it construed the meaning of innocence was so hopelessly one-sided. As I watched the film, I found myself repeating again and again in my mind, "I didn't do it!"

But leave innocence aside for a moment. What would it mean for a Muslim to feel like that in the face of terror?

What path could a Muslim person tread between between terror and peace? Supposing that was possible, how would you describe that tortuous path? Could you claim that they were, in fact, two separate paths? And assuming you could, could you convince yourself to believe in all that? Suppose you were Muslim and found yourself face to face with a female suicide bomber who'd been caught before detonating her bomb and making tomorrow's headlines; how would you respond? Would condemning her solve anything? And when people condemned her, was that any guarantee that they were being any more democratic than anyone else? Whenever problems arose, problems that could actually be easily solved if a group of people got together to discuss them, why was it only Muslims who had to pay for sorting out the mess and take sides when things spun out of control?

"You cannot escape the truth." That's what someone said in the documentary: "You cannot escape the truth." At that point I completely lost it. Instead of thinking it over, instead of breaking down in sobs or pulling into myself, leaving the world behind, instead of going on a long walk, stringing together statements of rebellion in the face of the senselessness of our experiences, I began to laugh. It was a strangled laughter that came from some unknown place in my being, even transcending me, and I laughed so hard that tears poured from my eyes. I hadn't laughed so hard since my arrival in DC. No, it wasn't just that; I hadn't laughed like that for months, for years. On the computer screen in front of me, against a background of rising flames, Zahide and the other three detainees were reading a fatwa, saying that those who strayed from the path of Allah would eventually get the punishment they deserved. I'd never seen Zahide like that; she looked as if she was weighed down with suffering. However, in the face of such sorrow, I had the same physical reaction: strangled tearful laughter.

Eventually, the three elderly men in the reading room snapped at me because I was laughing so much. The oldest of them growled at me, "This is a reading room, not a laughing room!"

I had no other choice but to pack up my things and leave. But even that I couldn't properly manage. I dropped my bag on the floor, fumbled as I put on my coat, got my scarf tangled up in the arms of the chair, and had a difficult time getting the documentary to shut down on my computer. And the whole while I kept bursting into laughter. I had the urge to turn to the three men in the room and recite one of those lines from the film, lines that Richard had probably wanted his characters to memorize: "Look here, evil ones! You shall be damned to hell for straying from the path of God. That's why we are here, to show you that!"

But of course I didn't say anything. I left behind the noises of the library, its coughs and sneezes occasionally interrupted by the sound of violins. But when I walked out the door, I could go no further. I collapsed onto a bench at the entrance of the library, feeling another explosion of laughter welling up within me, but this time there were shrieks as well. The storm raging within me had grown in intensity, but all the same, I froze up with a strange sense of calm.

Deep within me, a different voice had arisen, a different kind of revolt. The strange thing, however, was that I felt a sense of belonging. To what and whom, and why? I had no point of reference. Yet again, it was a rush of irrational feelings. In those years, had I ever been able to explain my own emotions to myself? Were they even truly my own?

Another wave of laughter broke loose and tears rolled down my cheeks as I rocked backwards and forwards, trying not to fall off the bench. I was left dazed by all that laughter. Somehow that strange film had unexpectedly changed something in me. The film summarized the last twenty years of Zahide's life, from her childhood to her life in America up to the time when she was whisked away in an operation and flown off to New York, where she was tortured and dragged from prison to prison and then into the unknown. Just seeing her in that film, which seemed to slip between reality and fantasy, left me stunned, feeling as though I were in a drunken stupor. It was quite strange, as though I'd found yet another reality in that propaganda-laden film, a silenced world of degradation, humiliation and ridicule. I was profoundly moved; it spoke to the meaninglessness and emptiness I carried within. Is that what I'd been craving for such a long time? I felt like I'd found the answer, a fiction of some kind that spoiled the meaning I'd been living through and seeking out. They say that if you search for meaning, you'll be crushed under its weight. And the same holds true if you search for virtue; it will crush you, just as you'll be buried under the weight of truths you seek out, as I'd been crushed in my search for Zahide as I found out more about her. Yet I felt that after such a long time, I was able to breathe again.

As I searched for Zahide for those two years I felt like I was trying to find my own lost family. Although it was a search for nothingness I persevered and the result was anything but surprising: nothingness echoed with nothingness. And for some, that might be a choice. What did I decide? To go on. At the graveside of my husband and son, I was freed from everything that weighed upon me when I bid them farewell and spurned my own death. While some may find such an attitude selfish, that was the line I drew between living and dying. Maybe that was a point on which I was in agreement with Richard: We, as the living, are incapable of understanding reality and thus cannot comprehend the details of death and all it entails, not to mention the utter meaninglessness of it all. That held true as we wandered through life in such mediocre ignorance, spreading our existence ever so thin; that held true no matter how hard we tried to understand the secret of the universe by concocting experiments and formulas.

That film had rent asunder the veil of meaning that hung between Zahide and myself, reminding me of the importance of cause-and-effect relationships. We had to accept certain things the way they were. Zahide had either deserved to disappear or perhaps she just decided to do so. Accepting things as they are affords a certain comfort.

War, on the other hand, was a reality that we couldn't turn away from. But even war offers us a means of escape. And it was precisely that notion in that contrived documentary that made me burst into laughter.

It was the nothingness of everything. That nothingness was so tangible that whoever watched the film would have no choice but to laugh, as though following a laugh track on a television show. It wasn't a laughter of relief, but it did me good.

No matter how much I denied it, that was Richard's success! What's more, it was the counterpart that would be at hand when the New Conservatism he praised had spread all around the world. Actually, war was real for just one side in the standoff. A war of civilizations . . . It was a genuine polarization. However, the documentary offered a different angle, which was that this new war, which went beyond ideological causes and would get caught up in cultural disintegration, wasn't in fact real. It was a question of whether it was a war that existed between the Richards and Zahides in the world. It seemed as though it was my own personal war, a war of choice in which fear, anxiety and suspense flowed. A war of distinguishing right from wrong—as if there were, in fact, such a thing as right and wrong.

It was a war of spectators in which ignorance tried to vindicate itself with conscience, conscience with action, action with ways of naming and describing, and in the end, each once was defeated by the other. It was, at best, a war of the witness. Or perhaps it wasn't Zahide or Richard's war at all. Not the war of the deep rift that opened up between civilizations, but of the witnessing that was to tumble into that void.

Zahide and Richard . . .

I had a strange feeling that told me it was a relationship that contained just enough romance and was thought-provoking beyond measure. As I sat on the bench, the snow seemed to be falling within me as well, pushing that feeling onward.

My feelings were right. The film and the ideas it promoted shifted to a different ground in light of the fifteen-minute clip we watched in class that depicted Zahide as a terrorist. That was an entirely different way of tackling the question of where the world is heading. But that angle was quite unbelievable. At best it had to be some kind of black humor, the kind that underpinned comical characters as cold laughter echoes in the background. That was the feeling it gave you. You laughed as you wept, becoming purified in the process. That is, you became as purified as you can be in the face of the vulgarity of the times. Seeking catharsis from a Greek chorus was an exercise in futility. There was nothing left to laugh or cry for. That was the price we paid for bearing witness to our battles. To our survival. To our push forward.

And I continued laughing, relentlessly. Not being able to ever know the truth was such a relief. Everything offered up to us was like the reality of the times: NONEXISTENT.

11

The fourth time that I met up with Zahide I could see that her mind had become warped. The interview was long and tiresome. As she spoke, she insulted me from time to time, saying that I was no different from the others who use her and that she said she knew that I was part of the game. She wasn't entirely wrong. Still, I denied it; I tried to deal with her anxiety and stress in an objective manner. She claimed I was a torturer, too. All the same, she told me her story, speaking with blithe indifference.

* * *

It began with a journey from Dulles to New York. December 2, 2001. If I'm Zahide Sohni Mühür, that journey happened. Yes, it happened dear criminologist, esteemed Mr. Expert. They've been drugging me since I arrived in the hospital. Richard is actually the one who's responsible for it all. It started with him. Although my mind may slip at times between reality and fantasy, I know that trip happened. I swear with God as my witness.

First, we walked from the departure lounge and then boarded the plane. I was handcuffed and blindfolded.

We approached the door of the plane. We could call it the Timberland door. Everyone was wearing Timberland boots.

Men and women, dressed in black.

Young people ready to die for their country.

The plane was like a huge boot. A Timberland boot. A yellow, slightly fuzzy thing. The Phoenix was waiting, ready for takeoff.

Phoenix. Simurgh. How could a mythical character ever become something so vile? A Phoenix, they say. How could a legend be so utterly destroyed? Which Mount Qaf would clutch such a bird to its bosom? When they told us the name of that stadium, I figured it all out. Mount Qaf Stadium. That was where all those Phoenixes of the CIA, those filthy luxury jetliners, take us. It takes us on its back and whisks us away to that place, that fairytale land.

They call it a Phoenix. But it's absurd!

We entered through the Timberland door.

It may seem funny now, but who do you think I saw when I first stepped on the plane? My father, my opinionated dead father, musician, adventurer, lover of Istanbul. Dead. That was none other than part of the Phoenix program.

"Come, come sit by me, don't be afraid," he said. Then he asked, "What have you seen of that American vileness?"

I was bewildered.

"They drug me all the time, so I don't notice much," I said, not very surprised to see him there.

"That means your mind isn't all there," he said.

"Not really, it's there, despite it all. But that's what worries me."

It was a completely nonsensical question, but all the same, I asked, "Are we in the present time?"

"The present time is only in your head. Just keep your eyes on the road. The road is what's important. We must always keep going forward," my father said.

Such a puzzle!

As the plane took flight, I sank into the leather seat which was the color of coffee with cream.

"I killed my children, Father," I said. "How could that have happened? What kind of reality is this?"

I began to cry.

He didn't say a word.

"It's all nonsense, Father," I said.

He didn't say a word.

"Why did all this happen? Why is this happening, Father?"

Not a word.

Clouds below us. At one point, I think I heard Karen's voice from a distance. "We'll be landing in half an hour, Sohni," she said.

I'm holding my father's hand. Cold. I'm in the seat, it is the color of coffee with cream.

"Why am I here?" I ask myself. The pain never subsides. I have no dreams; all I have is one singular reality, and that's me disappearing, and as I begin to vanish, a ghost appears—I don't know whether it's real or not—the ghost of my father. And there are the drugs, and Karen, she came with the drugs and sent the thought of flying first rushing through my veins, and from there all through my body.

"Sohni, my dear girl," my father says to me.

I inhale, breathing in the sharp scent of coffee mixed with cream.

That's my father, Mürşit, sitting next to me.

I know that the drugs play tricks on me, but still I was caught off-guard.

"Dad . . ."

He's holding a cup of coffee. Somewhere in my body, I seem to know about his aspirations, his hopes for the future. My mind? No. My mind has long been a crippled lump of flesh. I remember him holding my hand. The warmth of his hands. The knobs, knuckles and calluses of his hands.

It's as if my father and I are not heading towards captivity but drawing up to a late afternoon that is just beginning to grow warm. For a moment I feel energized, like I'm not on the brink of tumbling down into deep sleep. So long till his death! The trace of coffee on his upper lip seems so real.

"What do you want to experience, Sohni?" he asks me.

"Father, is there something I should miss in this world?"

He didn't say a word.

I had to answer the question myself.

"I've missed long sunsets," I say. "Kind sunsets. Not those filled with solitude, but sunsets that ring with laughter and human warmth. We saw so many sunsets together, Father. In those moments, I could hear the voices of my mother, my brothers and sisters and my grandmother. Sohni was filled with joy, and clothes were hung out to dry, blowing in the wind. And there was ... There was ..."

"There was what, Sohni?"

"And there was a washtub nearby."

"*Ghara* ... You don't remember it's called a ghara? That was one of the first words your mother taught me. Do you remember Sohni's real story?"

"No, I don't remember a single thing. Why don't you tell me?"

"Don't you remember that day, Sohni?"

"No, no. Not a thing."

"That day, you looked at the ghara, that ceramic washtub in the garden, and asked what it was. And I began to tell you the story. The sun was setting. I was drinking my coffee with milk. You were wearing a flowing orange and red sleeveless dress. You had just gotten over an illness, and your face was pale like it is now. You had a necklace around your neck and it gleamed in the sunlight. You don't remember that either?"

"No, no."

"I began to tell you the story, and you were swinging your legs very slowly and listening quietly."

Once upon a time in the Punjab there was a master potter named Tulla. Tulla had a very beautiful daughter. And the name of this beautiful girl, as luck would have it, was Sohni. Tulla and his wife brought her up with so much love and care that Sohni, ah Sohni, grew up to into a charming young woman whose beauty was known throughout the land. One day a merchant named İzzet happened to go to the little town where Sohni and her family lived. İzzet Bey had heard of Sohni's beauty, so he went to Tulla's shop. The moment he saw Sohni he fell in love with her. He went again and again to the shop just to see her and in the end he went broke because he bought pottery every time he went. But his yearning for Sohni continued to burn. Desperate, he offered to work for Master Tulla and the master potter agreed and took him on. Day by day İzzet and Sohni's love grew stronger and stronger. Soon, however, her family began to grow suspicious and they married Sohni off to a man named Dam.

"What about the ghara, Father? What happened to the ghara?"

He laughed. "Back then, you would ask me exactly the same thing when I got to that part of the story. Just like that, narrowing your eyes.

"I would tell you 'Be patient, Sohni.' People who don't know how to be patient will never understand life and its secrets. The ghara is the key point, my dear child. Now listen. İzzet Bey was hurt, and he thought of leaving. Of course, that's not how it ends. There was a river that cut through the middle of the village. He crossed to the other bank of the river, but his thoughts kept going back to Sohni. And Sohni always thought of him, pining away! Now, what happens next?"

"I don't know, Father!"

"İzzet swims across to the other side of the river every night. Stroke after stroke, he goes to his love. Every night. However, as luck would have it, one night a fish bites his leg. That's trouble for you, it just sneaks up. But does Sohni ever give up? She's the daughter of a master potter. She clambers into a tub of fired clay. What is the tub called? Guess, guess, guess? A ghara. Wait, don't keep saying 'but, but.' Just listen. This is a story. Sohni crosses the river that night in that the tub. She's so happy, so very happy. Then the next night. And another night. But her family notices that something is amiss. Oh, for the love of God! Master Tulla goes mad. He makes a new ghara, but this one isn't as strong. He switches the old tub with the trick one and Sohni, of course, doesn't know so she gets into the trick ghara and pushes off into the waves. And then just as she was halfway across, it happens. It happens, my dear daughter. It happens to the ghara, but actually it happens to Sohni. She doesn't know how to swim. The tub breaks apart, and the water rushes into her lungs. That's where the story ends."

"Is that Sohni's fate? Is that it? Father, what kind of story is that?"

Sohni is cold. Sohni misses a vase made of fired clay. Could she have such thoughts on a plane? She longs to see that ceramic vase in her lap when she opens her eyes. Then the Phoenix lands at New Jersey Teterboro Airport.

I'm cold. "Karen, I'm very cold," I say to the woman next to me. Is she really Karen?

"Don't worry," Karen says. "It's probably just a side effect of the drug. Actually, it's warm in the plane, Sohni. Too warm for you to notice."

New York, New York
Zahide wants to tell her New York story. At one time, she loved that musical. "I loved its music, Levent Bey."

At the airport they put me on a van. I continue on this journey with my steel handcuffs, shackles, and fetters. I'm half asleep, curled up on van's rough floor. I ask them not to put on the blindfold again. I see clouds through the van's side windows and signs flashing past. Up above, the planes come and go. I catch sight of them for a moment, and then they are gone, heading towards their destinations.

The van passes down large avenues, passing by smaller streets. The signs still tell Sohni where she is. She has no historical memory. No trace of the past in those avenues and streets. But years ago Sohni had had to live in that city for a while. For a very short while. She still remembers some things. As she remembers, the dictionary meaning of "short" is emptied of meaning. She dreams of Emel. For a moment. The earthquake in 1999. She sends her all those letters afterwards, but never gets a reply. For her, New York mostly means Emel. She doesn't know why, but she misses her very much at that moment. Is it because she'll never see her again? She thinks of writing to the newspaper Emel worked for. And when a reply comes, she's stunned.

Zahide is out of breath. She's surrounded by corpses. "If only this were a lie," she says. "Perhaps is it I who am dead." She can't tell which one is real. She misses lies, tales, legends. Legends in which time shuttles backwards. Tales in which everyone changes places. Immortality . . .

For days, the word "Emel" stirs something deep inside her. Again and again she relives in her mind the time she saved Emel from drowning. The breath she gave her. Memories. Their conversations in Turkish and Urdu. How quickly Emel picked up Urdu. When she hears those old expressions that crop up in Sohni's Turkish, Emel laughs: "What's that," she says, "is it something from the Orkhon inscriptions?" For days, Zahide is filled with a burning desire to relive those memories.

What about now? Through different eyes, she sees New York where she'd last seen her. Who's alive, who's dead? She's lost the thread. She doesn't know anything else.

The van moves, wheezing in that city of madness. Stop at the lights, stop in the traffic. Moving is perhaps the wrong word, because they are stuck in traffic all the time. Every once in a while, the van is shaken as a few techno junkies bump into the van as they walk by. That mad city belongs to them and them alone. That's the only movement—the van shaken as the techno junkies pass by.

Someone says, "They let all the lunatics go free in New York."

Zahide knows that voice, but she can't remember whose it is.

"These people won't start any revolutions or light a fire in the middle of the street. But not to worry! They're a solid bunch. They fill the city with life, filling it up. Those people are the revolution themselves. How else would life be filled up? Life is filled by living it. Huh? Wake up. You're just another junkie to us now. That's why I'm afraid of you. Whoever said you should be included in the Theta Project? I didn't say anything. In any case I'm an invisible man. I have no influence. But I'm afraid of those lunatics out there. If I had a chain, I'd lock myself to those shackles of yours. Shackles bear a certain weight these days. They have a value and a weight. Don't fall sleep. Oh, those lunatics ... You always have to be on the alert. Look at that street; nothing's moving. Almost everyone is in a state of distraction. Fickle is another name for this city. You eat a hot dog and you go back. You're a fanatic for speed, but the road wears you out."

A few more people bump past the van.

"Zahideee?"

The bouncing echoes in Sohni's ears like that. Someone is calling her Zahide. That's the same voice from a moment ago.

Another bump.

"Do you remember that night, Zahide? You were at our house in Queens. The place was filled with those flying cockroaches that scare you so much. And how they leapt! Drum roll, tom-tom, cymbal. Still, you insisted on sleeping on the floor. You had a friend with you that night. Do you remember? Her name was Emel."

"Emel? Yes."

"Yes, her."

"But who are you?"

"For God's sake, I'm Yusuf, don't you recognize me?"

"Yusuf?"

"You and Emel and I had a class together. I played the saxophone."

"Yusuf from Jordan!"

"That's right, Yusuf from Jordan. That summer I went to New York to make some money. I was going to play at a nightclub, but it didn't work out. I took a break from school and worked as a limousine driver for a while. That was around the time you came to our place. I guess your husband had come to New York or something. Or maybe you were about to get married. He called you that night, don't you remember? He was staying somewhere in Long Island. Secret stuff, you see. You, Emel, and I took the train together. A station wagon met us at the station. The car had a flat tire or something and you went crazy and started yelling like a madwoman. What was your husband's name? Dam, Dam. I had a lot of fun that night, calling him Van Damme. But you were furious. You said that you didn't want that man named Dam. You shouted at Dam's friend who was driving the station wagon and called him a jackass. You asked what right he had to intrude in your life. And Dam's friend just stared, giving us dirty looks. Then you got in the station wagon. You sat in the back and looked back at us through the window. It was terribly sad. We stood there stunned, dumbstruck. Why the hell did you marry that man named Dam?"

"I remember now. That night you had your sax with you. We had such a good time at your place in Queens until Dam called!"

"You were wearing a chain necklace back then, too. I remember now, Zahide. You were wearing an orange and red dress, like this color. You came to New York and said that they let the lunatics go free in this city. The city wore you out. But later you grew to like New York. Central Park, all the people running amok. And the gambling dens and sham glances in Manhattan during half-day tours. It was a three- or four-day thing, do you remember, Zahide? The twin towers. But now, we better not mention that."

"I remember that house. An ice cream vendor would pass by a block or two away, right?"

"Yes, you're probably right."

"You made up a melody for it. *Eh, kadi na Sohni tor carche di.*"

"Exactly! I remember the rhythm now."

"You played it to us on your sax. But it was the ice cream man's rhythm first: *Ah, Sohni, your love will never bud.*"

"The name of the song was 'Ghara.' One night you said to Emel, 'You're my Ghara.' Then you told us the story of the Ghara. We wrote that song together: *Ghara is a close, close friend/If anyone, she'll be the one to carry you across the river/But there is impossibility in everything, Sohni/Our destinies have been written/And that's what becomes of our lives.*"

"There's a song like that, Yusuf. It was written by Nusret Fateh Ali Khan."

Yusuf mentions his admiration for Nusret Fateh Ali Khan. On the second floor of a two-story house in Queens: Yusuf, Emel and her.

"What did you girls do today?" Yusuf asks.

"We went to Brooklyn."

"What did you do?"

"We walked around."

"Do you know," Yusuf says, "there's a major detention center in Brooklyn."

"But why?" Emel asks. "Why would they put one in the middle of the city?"

"Gulags are everywhere these days. We're surrounded by them," Yusuf says.

"What do they do there?" Emel asks, suddenly curious.

"That's the last stop for immigrants. Then they're deported."

Deportation

The van stopped in the heart of the city. They picked Zahide up, as if hugging her, and took her half-dead body straight to the center.

They undid her chains and put her in a cell.

Twenty-four hours. When it's truly lived, it seems like a lifetime.

The fed her foul McDonald's hamburgers. Beef, pickles, ketchup, mayonnaise. Cold sleep, deep sleep.

Somewhere underground, where an entire day became entangled with the night, where the night left its mark on the day and was cleared of blame, Sohni listened to the sounds of the city. There were lonely, despondent people who didn't know, and didn't want to know, the history that unfolded and didn't want to ascribe meaning to those moments. They knew that even if they wanted to, it was no longer necessary. That was a place where it seemed that life outside was based on the idea, "God, they know not what they do" and then subtly shifts to "God, is it a sin or not?" Quietly shrouded in her own variegated colors.

As if under a spell, she listened to herself breathe in and out, inhaling the dust rising up from the buildings collapsing in the middle of the city, listening to each collapsing building demolishing more magic in her memories. And she listened, helplessly, to the power of change.

Sohni listened. She listened to the commercials, sitcoms, news and stories about solitary children raiding schools. For a while, she was haunted by the loneliness fired from the barrels of their guns, and then she listened again: how to avoid colon cancer, young geniuses, marathons to be held on Sundays. There were halls of loneliness in libraries scattered around the city, and in one library an elderly person berates another for speaking on the phone. There is that, and much worse. She listened to the elderly cursing at each other at Alzheimer's clinics, a young Chinese man vomiting at the street corner and the song he sang—it could have been a scene from a movie—and then there were people jogging for their health, therapists, life coaches, weather forecasts, Rice's upcoming piano recitals, and on and on. She watched commercials leap from light beams and television screens. She listened to the people on the streets who talked to themselves. All alone they went to Mexican restaurants to try some spicy fast food, something new. She listened to them. NGOs and the mayor would condemn Taco Bell because a mouse had been seen in the drive up window. It was the end of Taco Bell, and she listened to that too. Chic Pot would fill in the gap in the market, and Latinos would land the jobs that no one else would take, working for a pittance. She listened.

To the cab drivers who wouldn't pick up anyone in the rain. And to her songs, to "Ni Sohni-e."

To the cashier who said everything had changed since 9/11.

Sohni listened to everything. The pleasant things and the hideous. Everything couldn't be all that bad, she thought, it simply couldn't be. No one would make eye contact with you, and that was a good thing.

You could be alone while dying, that's why.

No, you shouldn't be cynical. A man said that in a sitcom.

Then Sohni listened to the birds.

On the porch of her house in Kensington she listened to the birds, to the rustling bamboo plants lining the porch, to the creak of their stems under the weight of the snow. One morning when she woke up with her two sons there was three feet of snow—three feet!— they ran into the yard and built the biggest and most meaningful snowman in their lives, even if it were the least shapely.

Meaning?

Sohni listened to what meaning is.

The bamboo teetered.

The birds chirped.

Monsters blew their whistles.

No one looked at you; no one cared.

She realized she wasn't afraid. The snowman melted as though with a hiss.

İzzet shouted, "It's all melted!"

"Don't worry, İzzet," Sohni said. "We'll make another one."

"But Mom, there's no snow!"

"Don't worry," she said to İzzet.

Sohni listened. She listened only to listen, not to seek out evidence of her existence. Not to prove herself, not at all. She didn't have to prove herself to anyone. Not to anyone or to anything.

In that place where the day becomes entangled with the night and the night with the day.

Sohni was kept waiting under a light that shone a singular color. She had more than enough time to take full advantage of the restrictions imposed on her and the verbal and physical abuse meted out by her guardians.

Time came.

Time went.

Sohni slept through all of the tumult.

When she was awakened towards morning, her fate would to be the same as the other detained immigrants. Hands bound, she would be ordered to sit in a chair and read a script written on a piece of white paper.

She would be deported—Sohni Zahide Mühür. Clearly she deserved it. The tone of the man who read the paper confirmed it. Every word he read was like a slap in the face. She was found guilty of aiding and abetting Al-Qaeda. She was guilty of being from a "third-world" country. She was guilty of believing in a different religion. She was even guiltier for attempting it as a woman. In the eyes of the man reading these lines, she was as ignorant as can be. She'd been doomed by birth. She was inept. And in any case, what did she know?

Sohni listened. She listened to the accusations as she would have listened to the rustle of the bamboo.

"You'll be sent to Sweden, then to Syria through Jordan," the man said.

Sweden?

Sohni didn't even ask. She didn't even ask herself.

The Sohni that the man saw, and all the others like her, would have to listen.

Then the guards beat her, delivering blunt, heavy rib-breaking blows.

On the road to Amman,

Zahide says, "Medications. There were only drugs, Levent Bey."

More drugs.

After landing in Sweden and picking up two Egyptian detainees, the Phoenix landed in Jordan at three in the morning.

Sohni was blindfolded, her hands were cuffed, and then she was put in a car.

The trip took around forty-five minutes.

She was placed in one of numerous huts spread out in an empty field. She was asked a few basic questions, but never really replied.

She was slapped and beaten, and then raped by the guards a couple of times. She felt nothing.

In the afternoon, she was shoved into the car again and after about an hour arrived at the Syrian border. That was her adventurous journey to Damascus. Then they drove over an old railroad track. A conversation took place between her and Yusuf at that time.

Yusuf has a book in his hand. But I can't possibly tell what it is. "Can you guess," he asks, "what the subject is?" I don't understand anything. I hum my mother's songs on the bank of a river. Yusuf smiles like a child. "Look," he says. "This is US Immigration Law."

"Yusuf, you're dead," I say. "I will also die soon."

"I'm quoting it to you word for word," Yusuf insists, "US officials have been given some pretty broad authority with regards to who will be deported and how. However, that shouldn't mean that those officials have the same infinite authority to send someone to a place where they'll likely be tortured."

"Drop all this nonsense. Tell me something about life."

"About life? It's been a long time since I died!"

"So, tell me anyway," I say.

"I died in the rendition program. I wasn't as innocent as you. I had some sort of connection with that Van Damme of yours. I mean, that's what they said. They made me sign a document saying that. That's all there was left of my life, just an official document. What more can you ask! Not everyone is privileged to die so officially."

"But that's not possible," I say. "You and Van Damme?"

"For you, nothing is ever possible," Yusuf says.

"It's just not possible," I repeat.

"They held me in the Palestinian camp in Syria for ten months, and then one day, during the torture, that was it. Dead."

"That can't be," I say with mock incredulity. I have no idea why.

"Anyway, listen to me. Prepare yourself. They will torture you with electric shocks. Be prepared for all kinds of psychological torment. The worst is solitude. Don't forget that. You won't see anyone for ten months or so. Never mind me saying ten months, you'll be alone the whole time within the confines of your own mind. That will be a very long time indeed."

The sentence "You'll be alone" becomes lost among the secrets of life, accompanied by the sound of a saxophone.

Zahide sees Yusuf more clearly.

"My God, Zahide, don't you remember that we played a game at the house in New York? What was it called, give me a minute . . ."

"Clue."

"Yes!"

"Do you remember the name of the inspector, Zahide?"

"No, I can't remember what it was."

"The guy's name was Richard!"

"Richard! He was my neighbor in Kensington. Unbelievable!"

"He was your true killer, Zahide. He was a nutcase working on the FBI's Theta Project. He was his father's Frankenstein. He writes eulogies for the dead in the Metro supplement of the *Washington Post*. It's like he's trying to create some kind of bond with the dead because he couldn't do it with the living."

"No, you must be confusing him with someone else. He was my neighbor."

"Your neighbor and your executioner!"

"It's all a game," Zahide said. "I still remember the board of that game we played."

"Richard had a house with flowers in the yard, tall spindly flowers."

"The house next door had a beautiful yard."

"Yes, a paradise of chrysanthemums."

"Those were the best three days of my life, Yusuf."

"Those were the best three days of my life, Zahide."

At that moment, the car will turn left on Chance Street.

"Just like in the game, Zahide. Chance Street."

"That was just a game," Zahide will say. "It's just too much, I give up!"

"Everything's a game," Yusuf will say.

They'll go through the first intersection and turn right at the second intersection onto Palestine Street. Then they must take the first right. A broad square will be awaiting them there and they will approach a massive building that is surrounded by armed soldiers. Then they'll come to a black gate, through which they will pass and find themselves in a courtyard.

From the courtyard, Zahide will be taken into the building. She'll be interrogated and threatened for five hours in a small room. The next day, she'll be taken down to the basement of the building where she'll be placed in cell number 5. Indeed, Zahide will stay in that cell for ten months. In her own words, she'll endure the worst of all tortures in that hellhole.

A cell,

35 inches wide,

70 inches long,

80 inches high.

The walls were concrete and the floors made of red brick. All they'd given me was a blanket, two plastic bowls, and two bottles, not to mention the rats.

"How could I go on staying here without dying?" Zahide asked Yusuf. However, Yusuf was long gone. How could you endure that darkness, that coffin, without losing your mind?

Just then she would discern a real silhouette in the darkness. Karen. The syringes. The distance.

"Hello, Sohni," Karen said. "It's time for you to relax."

"Yusuf, Father, where are you?" the prisoner shouted.

No sound, no light. If anything, there were screams in the distance.

"Torture.

Why don't you try telling me about the torture?" That's what I asked. She stared at me blankly. As if to say, "What are you talking about, Levent Bey!" Then she stood up and began pacing.

Three square feet or a quarter of an inch, what difference does it make? Sohni thought.

She was in a world where she knew she'd be woken up every hour on the hour. A world that she'd register with lapses in her perception of it, divided by what she thought was every hour, a world split up into pieces. She could think of a separate story for every quarter of an inch. An incorrect story. An invisible, inaudible, imperceptible, miserable fiction, every quarter of an inch of which must be thought out at the cost of responsibilities for the past. Despite that, a group of entireties that somehow need to be designed and approved. That was life, an ensemble where it was hoped that each moment would be shaped based on the previous one. She was there because she had to pay the price for what she'd done before. And someone would have to pay for those moments, whether it was Sohni or someone else. Time, which was divided into hours as the light flooded her cell every hour on the hour, was nothing more than the price she had to pay for each quarter of an inch and every split second.

In a space of three square feet she would wait. Her body had been transformed into a timing device more sensitive than any clock they had. And it ran on waiting, not electricity. At one time, however, life had meant seeking something out.

She'd wait. For the moment they'd arrive, for the moment they'd insult her, for every refraction of light filling her cell, in that quarter-of-an-inch break when darkness meets the light. Sohni used to seek out that moment when the darkness pressed up against twilight and moved towards the light, because at that very moment her very self fell away. She was neither a prisoner nor a guard, neither Muslim nor Christian. She was in a place where she was all or none of those. In that sliver of time, a spacing moment.

That's what happened when the darkness was severed by light. Faces covered, the guards would say:

"Hey, what's up, Sohni?"

Those were their first words.

The darkness would speak of a completely different woman, a woman from the past, and whisper of the light, of Sohni.

And one of those times, she wouldn't know what to say to the brute force that filled her cell not with light but with the rattle of chains and insults. The fact that her hands were handcuffed behind her back would not be enough for them. That her feet were chained to the cell floor was never enough. Their power was immense. It was a shameless power, wielded by six or seven people. One of them sounded familiar.

Karen?

"Get up, Al-Qaeda slut!"

"Dirty whore!"

And someone was spitting in her face.

Sohni was trying to protect her head. The chains clattered.

She winced.

It seemed as if the chain was yelling in Urdu, "Admit it!"

Confess! But what?

Sohni didn't know what to admit, or where and when to do so on this journey to the land of the dead. As always, she'd say "I admit it all," and they wouldn't believe it. Admitting it all actually meant admitting nothing. Yet there it was, the secret of all the torture she was put through. Admitting it all meant that almost everything was pulled from that singular moment. In the same way, admitting little by little, breaking it all down into pieces and admitting by dissociating from it meant breaking down, being mentally exhausted, disappearing.

They took from her every page that corresponded with her life.

If every stage meant a memory, Sohni had exhausted them all.

Each stage meant the end of a magic spell that belonged to her.

In the end, all Sohni had left to say was, "I admit it all." The final point of resistance.

All her memories and her past were torn to shreds and she became a mere silhouette on this journey to the realm of death.

There's blood.

The coffin bleeds. The floor is wet. The walls bleed. The final words bleed. The world bleeds, it bleeds as it comes to an end.

There's blood.

There's no sound, no light. There are prisoners of rendition subjected to torture. Strangled cries. If you tried hard, you could mistake those cries for laughter. It could be a woman gathering up laughter, just like in that song.

12

Cries are sometimes like laughter.
At times the woman who scoops up laughter
Gathers up pain and sorrow
In place of laughter and joy.

"What's that from, Zahide?" She had been mumbling that verse over and over.

"My dear Emel, it's just an old thing," she said.

Fog enveloped us. There was still much to be lived. That's why we were young. But at the same time, we were old because we'd aged so much.

Zahide had graduated, but I had to study all summer. We went to New York for three days. Yusuf, an Arabic teacher in our department, worked there during the summer. Zahide was planning on starting a new life by marrying Dam, the suitor her uncle thought would be suitable for her. There was no hope, no expectations, no future. Only laughter, and lots of it. Yusuf said he would host us in the house he shared with one of his musician friends in Queens. The summer was hot, like in all remembrances of the past. There was no end to the insects that crawled around on the floor of the house, they just kept coming and coming. Had we known we were going to stay in such an odd-smelling house, I don't think we would have accepted the invitation. Everything in the house was infused with a dingy smell and the entire place was infested with bedbugs. Yet those three days would bring us such child-like joy, and rather than linger on impending farewells, we set off for New York. That jar full of laughter spilled open on our seventeen-hour train ride, which was like a premonition of the next three days to come that would change everything.

The train passed through deserts, old cities, and plains, occasionally skirting the shores of lakes. I don't exactly know why, but that train ride somehow summed up what we'd become in America. An equation opened up before us, the unforgettable intricacies of which you would never be able to see from a plane. While we knew that flying was actually safer, travelling by train was more alluring, even though we didn't have much time. And perhaps part of that allure was the fact that we didn't have much money, so we decided to disregard the admonitions of risk statistics and take the train. At the risk of our humdrum, synthetic American lives, nearly every aspect of which could be measured, fractioned and proportioned, we tried to blow a gaping hole in that "charmed" table of statistics. That didn't mean we were challenging the ways of life of the majority, or trying to cut it short, transforming it into a prefix or suffix. Not by any means. We were simply two women in a vast country where inductive methods could be applied without regret and we could confidently surrender ourselves to the future. We found ourselves in a country where intelligence was the basis of all competition, and we'd begun to vanish. Society seemed to say, "Oh, you mean intelligence? Well, that's merely physiological. The statistical data concerning the criteria of upbringing are indicated in the table." That was our main problem. The distances were unimaginable, a fact that the train made more explicit. The spaces were vast. Outer space was out there. And annihilation.

That's how we passed through the deserts. When the fog began rolling in, Zahide abruptly admitted, "You know, Emel, I don't feel like a Pakistani most of the time."

That statement didn't need canned laughter. It was sincere. We smiled to ourselves at the sadness stirred by what she said.

Zahide then asked, "Have I told you about the song of the woman who gathers laughter?"

"No."

"My late mother used to sing that song. There once was a woman who, throughout her life, gathered the laughter of the people she loved into jars. The song says that when we cry, laughter comes out with the tears."

"How so?"

"Because we make the same sounds in grief and joy."

"That's rather philosophical."

"Indeed."

We both looked out the window. The fog also seemed to be a desert. I wondered how the woman had gathered laughter, how she detached it from time, space and bodies. I asked Zahide. "I don't know," she replied. All she knew was that her mom loved that song and when she sang it with her dad, her eyes sparkled with joy.

Zahide talked for a while about her past, describing Karachi, where she was born. She talked about the eagles that invaded the city and the rats upon which they fed. The sewers had long been a problem in Karachi, and that was where the rats thrived. Then she told me about how her mother and father had become important figures in the Pakistani music industry and that their song "Eagles and Rats," would ultimately cost them their lives.

I began to see Zahide's life not as a vision, like infinity extending out beyond us, but as a momentary image that flashed through a train window. Perhaps I thought that because my own perspective was so commonplace. But still, Zahide had a way of brushing over matters of great consequence as if they were trifles.

"The soldiers killed my parents. My brothers and sisters were sent into exile."

Her manner of speaking made it sound like she was merely describing the particularities of a character in a novel. She depicted her own childhood like a noon shadow cast over a roof, lost in an unknown desert. With the same calm, she said it had been decided that it would be best if she went to stay with her uncle and aunt who lived in the US after she finished school. In any case, that was the only option she had. But I realized that the problem was not with her cursory way of summarizing tragedies. It was actually about the fact that she no longer felt like a Pakistani. The sentence fell from her lips once, and then once again, and then vanished into the desert along with everything else she said.

The real issue was about that feeling of being crushed—she herself was miniscule in the face of such a vast country—as she struggled to come to terms with and make sense of it all: her religion, language, past, painful memories, and above all, her country. If she pushed it a little further, I have no doubt that Zahide would have had no qualms with saying she felt like an American, like the rush of a powerful river. Perhaps it was the calm of the desert that made her open up. She had been living in that country, which once seemed so foreign to me, for the last ten years. When seen from another direction, such as the east or south, the paradoxes that arise there produce such humor, but a strange kind. She had come to the realization that the humor that comes from those paradoxes, and the point of view that goes along with it, are America's life blood; in short, for her America was no longer mere distant dreams that generated themselves again and again, filtered by a mind on the other side of the ocean. For

Zahide, it had become the embodiment of those very dreams. It was a land where anything could happen, whether excess, fantasy or annihilation.

"Do you know the difference between being a Pakistani and being an American, Emel?"

All I could muster in response was: "What?"

"Our dreams and how we cherish them."

Again I was at a loss for words: "How?"

"We dream about the future and about the present, but we never quite get it right. In the name of the present, we have no heaven that we can offer either the world or ourselves. We're unconcerned about experiencing heaven in the present. Relentlessly we struggle with sorrow, pain, and grief."

"What's so wrong with that? We don't have any other choice."

"Yes, the world is full of war, and life is cruel. As we slide from hope to hopelessness, everything we do and expect from life is based on dreams that are always divided up for the future. Aside from desiring brighter days to come, what we're pursuing is not very beautiful."

"But Zahide, what is beauty anyway?"

We both looked out the window, gazing at the desert.

"What's beautiful is the present, Emel. This very moment. *Now* is beautiful, even if it promises nothing but monotony. That's why I care about this country. It's about the impartiality of its dreams, although at times they may be too domineering at times. I care about this place because it has discovered what not just what belongs to the future but the present. And by doing so, it has managed to bring fantasy into real life because it hasn't become indebted to the future. Its power comes from this flexibility it shows towards life, not because it possesses the most powerful weapons on earth."

"I think there's something that you're missing though, Zahide.

Even if I agree with you to a certain extent, this country's politics and political climate are really quite brutal at times."

"I'm talking about dreams, Emel. Do you know of any other country where dreams come true like they do here? Of course, I know what's behind the power that took my family from me. I'm just talking about dreams."

"In a way, you're right. But there is the danger that those dreams will someday create a present of their own brought about by military power. This is the nineties. We'll have to wait and see. It's my fear that the power of regular people's dreams will turn into the power of military dreams and phantoms. The huge military here isn't training for world peace. Soon, very soon, that dream will become a reality and it's going to be bloody as hell. You know that as well as I do. What's come over you?"

Zahide turned and looked at me.

"Perhaps I'm just exhausted, Emel. Perhaps my dream is just that—being on a porch, my legs stretched out, thoroughly taking in the moment with no conditions whatsoever.

"Oh my. I think you have a case of wedding jitters."

"Maybe," she smiled. "I have a jar in which I gathered my laughter for you. I'll give it to you when it comes time for us to say goodbye," she said. Her face was like a blurred mirage in the vastness of the desert.

For weeks after I watched Richard's film, the memory of that mirage of Zahide's face tormented me. In the meantime I was investigating the torture that had been carried out as part of the rendition program and looking into the testimonies that had been given by "suspects" under the influence of various drugs. Again I turned to the internet. As I feared, I didn't come across Zahide's name in any of the documents I found. The situation seemed hopeless, but then Nadir managed to get some crucial information from a criminologist he knew at Georgetown University. I'd heard about him before; his name was Levent Koryürek, and he was Turkish. Nadir and I found out at the last minute that he had actually worked on the rendition program. We took comfort in the fact that at last we'd had a stroke of luck, but soon we discovered that Levent Koryürek would soon be leaving for Istanbul and would stay there for a while to continue his work. I had no choice but to push for a chance to meet him, as I would never be content with whatever information Nadir might be able to get.

I'd become obsessed with the idea of tracking down Zahide, almost an illness. An obsessive illness. There are ailments that aren't obsessive as well, the kind that pass after a few months, not leaving a trace. But mine was nothing like that; my suffering just worsened as time went by. I could have decided just to let it go, and set myself adrift in the current of life. I could have just wiled away the time, watching sunrises and telling jokes. But that would have meant putting myself into an altogether different kind of mental space. Call it escape or what you will; if you can just let go, the suffering will subside. That's how it was for me, until I met Zahide. For her, there are certain steps and measures you have to take in life. Just thinking about them brings on defeat. But quite oddly, I embraced this inevitable defeat. It was a way of guarding against the pain.

"That's a reasonable justification," Nadir said. With that implication, he did everything in his power to arrange a meeting for me with Levent Koryürek, and once he agreed, there was no way I could get out of it. Levent Koryürek was a brilliant academic whose work life kept him busy as he attended conferences and panels and taught one seminar after another. But he didn't have the arrogance that was so typical of academicians. He was said to be an ambitious academic for whom advancement was a top priority, and as result he was quite sought after by the think tanks in DC. His work was closely followed by the Turkish government, and his liberal credentials had earned him acclaim as a young and competitive go-getter who legitimized his opinions with a rationale based on the notion that "the ends justify the means." It was said that his ideas would become a guiding force for the policies of the military, as well as for the Turkish and American governments and the Middle East as well. He apparently had close ties with the CIA, the American military, and the Democrats. In short, Levent Koryürek was destined to become an indispensable figure in the future, and rumor had it that he was a Mason.

We met on a Thursday afternoon, and I noticed that the snow had begun melting. Nadir joined us as well. My original goal was to try to put all the pieces together, to tease out the origins of the hallucinations I felt that I carried within, a phantom in the form of Zahide, who smiled and remained impossibly elusive. That's what I'd thought at the beginning of our conversation.

"Please call me Levent. Levent Bey is a little too formal," he began. Contrary to what I had expected, he was rather plain and modest, and I immediately felt quite at ease in his presence, as though I could open up about anything. Nadir told him about my interest in the rendition program and emphasized that I had come to an impasse on one certain point. Right then and there, I wanted to explain to him why I was stuck. Of course, that was neither the time nor the place for it, but I couldn't resist.

"Sometimes we get confused about times and places. That's a natural, human reaction. However, there's much more to Project Monarch than meets the eye, just so you know! Those projects can really play tricks on our minds."

As Levent talked about the torments that targeted the human mind in the rendition program, I told him that what he said reminded me of something about myself. I said, perhaps unknowingly, that we all were part, in some way or another, of strange and curious projects. That's when Levent jokingly made that statement about how we sometimes confuse times and places. For some time, I'd been grappling with Zahide's memories and worrying that the slipperiness of my sense of time and location could somehow lead me astray. My sole comfort was that this was nothing new and I'd grown accustomed to that state of being. But of course I didn't tell Levent that.

For a moment his expression seemed friendly, even though he wasn't smiling at the time. Speaking quietly, as though from the depths of sleep, he continued speaking, repeating the usual claims that were packaged for easy consumption, smiling the whole while. Although he had an accent, his English was impeccable. He paused and looked at me, and then asked in the same somnolent tone, "So, how would you describe that place?" He didn't ask about the possible connections between me and that place, and listened, shading his face with his hand as the bright winter sun shone down over his cap.

That day, at that moment, both he and I were different. I felt as though we somehow knew each other. Our smiles, the way we studied each other's expressions, hinted at some uncanny familiarity. I found myself drifting off in thought, trying to match up my memories with his face, as though there were refracted images of shadow and light deep in my mind that somehow matched. But there was no clear answer, because everyone and every place resembles one another.

Abruptly I said, "Haydarpaşa." Just at that moment a white service bus from Georgetown University drove past, seeming to run over the word that had just fallen from my lips. I felt breathless as if time were running out.

How could I possibly explain that feeling: as I looked upon the trees with their bare branches, miles away from Haydarpaşa, the Potomac River seemed to be transformed into the Sea of Marmara. It was a winter day, Thursday. It could have been any winter day or any Thursday in the world. In the past, present or future, it didn't matter.

"It's possible," Levent said. "As I said, we sometimes get confused about times." With a bright smile, he added, "In those days, the crimes were not always committed at times that seem logical. But, like I said, Project Monarch is quite complex!"

Nadir nodded knowingly and glanced at me as if he sensed the strange relationship emerging between Levent and I. There was an almost radiant glow. At first, I wasn't careful enough about making sure I didn't inadvertently provoke a confrontation between Levent and Nadir by being so open, so I tried to steer my bewildered thoughts back to what Levent was saying and focus on the conversation. Despite my efforts, much of what he said fell on deaf ears as reveries tugged at my thoughts, and later I would only clearly remember a few things that he said.

What I later recalled was that Levent became interested in the project—the Monarch Project—after concerns had been raised after the implementation of the rendition program. As he said, the brainwashing policy, known as the MK Ultra Project, was actually an advanced offshoot of Project Monarch. And the point to which it brought humanity was the ultimate encapsulation of our day and age: We were losing our minds.

Levent continued with an air of confidence and his usual modest style:

"Initiated around the 1960s, the project was further developed and used by the CIA after 9/11. But this time, they turned their attention to the most troublesome part of the project, which had never been actually put to use. That was known as Theta."

"Theta?"

The Theta Project. I'd heard of it, but couldn't make any connections between it and the rendition program.

"It was a program that investigated psychic phenomenon," Levent explained. Then he continued with synthetic calm, as though trying to keep his excitement in check:

"In short, the project was terribly dehumanizing. The Soviets had toyed with it for quite some time. You might have read about it, but probably only in science fiction novels. America didn't have an opportunity to implement the program back then. In the end it was cancelled because a neuroscientist, a German Nazi who immigrated to the US in the early 1950s and had been involved in the project, had literally taken his work home and carried out some experiments on his family, especially his children. Just in case you're interested, the neuroscientist later changed his last name to Shelton."

"Shelton?" Nadir and I asked at the same time.

"Yes," Levent said.

His voice made me think of the flowing of crystal clear water.

I mulled it over: Could Richard actually be the son of that mad doctor?

There might be a connection, I thought, or it could just be coincidence. There were probably thousands, hundreds of thousands of Sheltons in the world.

"Anyway," Levent went on, "Theta lay dormant for quite a long time. However, the Soviets had achieved a lot with a similar project, so the Theta Project still held a certain appeal."

"I'm still a little unclear about what exactly happened. What kind of agents are they trying to create?" Nadir exclaimed.

Levent cut in: "They're hoping to develop agents who have the ability to read minds."

"Like a clairvoyant?"

Although I had asked the question, it seemed like someone else had uttered the words.

"No, fortune-telling is quite naive in comparison. This is highly scientific. I'm talking about reading brain waves, not soothsaying or foresight."

"Where can it go from there?"

"Frankly speaking, we know that some of the people taken in under the auspices of the rendition program were tortured to death wherever they were taken, and we know that some were sent to Guantánamo. But it's possible that quite a few of them were included in the Theta program in special facilities. We'll see the consequences of this maltreatment more clearly in the next ten or fifteen years. But in the end, the aim was to deploy an entirely new kind of agent by forcing them to undergo psychical treatments that would ostensibly give them the power to sense others' thoughts. And without a doubt that will change the way that we think about crime in the future."

"A new totalitarian regime is on its way, isn't it?" Nadir asked.

"Beyond the shadow of a doubt," Levent said.

Nadir pushed the issue: "How can they be so sure that the people they put through the program won't remember anything later?"

"There are codes, mostly in Latin. A different code is assigned to each agent, and only one or two other people know it. The code activates a chip that was implanted in the agent's body. How can I describe it? Think of it like magnetic doors. The only way they those doors to the memory can be opened is with those codes."

"Why should remembering the past be an issue? Why would an

agent like that even want to remember the past? And why would you want that to happen in the first place?"

"You can think of it as clearing out storage space to make room for new uploads. Because I'm not very technically inclined, every time I want to upload a new song to my son's iPod, I have to upload the entire playlist from the computer for that one song my son wants. The Theta program works the same way. It's a lot more difficult than you'd think to store information in the human brain, much less remove and improve it. That's the only way you can really get into a human mind from the outside."

My curiosity was piqued, and I couldn't stop myself from blurting the question, "And what about the stadiums?" That was probably the second time during the conversation that I'd said something quite foolish, after my comment about fortune-telling. Aside from that, it was rather remarkable how calm and composed I'd been.

"Ah yes, the stadiums. Indeed they do exist, Emel. The test subjects are revived in special facilities that are located seven stories beneath stadiums that have been specially built for the program. But it's a different kind of revival. And while no one has openly declared that they are using such facilities, stadiums will have a special place in programs undertaken by subcontractor countries which have agreements with the United States in the future. And you are Turkish, so this should interest you. There's even such a stadium in Istanbul."

"What!" I said in disbelief. Or perhaps it was more like, "Whaaaat?" One was an exclamation, the other a question. Either way, my despair at the idea was evident.

But aside from that, when I interrupted Levent I felt a powerful urge to revolt rush through me. I didn't want to just rise up against what he had just said, but the entire system that had been put into motion. He was talking about the serious maltreatment of human beings, but he talked about it in the most offhand manner imaginable. Perhaps that was the secret of his tolerant patience: sheer indifference! He was like a strategist who tells you that something is amiss and then tells you how to fix it. He was a likeable enough strategist, but the content of what he was saying was simply inhuman.

And hence my cry of revolt. A cry of desperation.

I couldn't imagine such stadium prisons as being part of the skyline of Istanbul. In the refractions of my memories, that was being reflected from the past to the present—omnipresent detention and confinement, darkness, cells and endlessness. My cry of "What!" was a howl of revolt against that. And beneath that were recollections of my readings about testimonies of torture. The infamous Dark Prison, ear-splittingly loud songs by Eminem, beatings that became increasingly brutal as time went by. "What" was the sum total of it all, whisperings about mono-lithic ideals and a state made up of monotypic people, absorbed by the minds of people who would be revived seven stories under a stadium. The question "what" spoke of the hopes that were rent asunder by the unexpected.

Hope?

Hope was a light that could be discerned through the bars of a prison cell. A light turning gray. A gray spark that dimmed under the enormous white lights of the stadium. Silence that blended in with the roar of the crowd.

Levent continued on, as though he were giving a mere weather report:

"Rumor has it that stadiums with such facilities will be used not just in Istanbul but in some other cities in Turkey, too. And it's not just Turkey. In the rendition program, people with exceptional intelligence are assigned stadium duties. And that means working on programs that will contribute to a megaproject in the future. However, before that happens, I'm sure of one thing: those people have been nothing more than guinea pigs for the Theta project. Afterwards they undergo plastic surgery, just like people in witness protection programs, to keep their identities concealed. But Emel, there's an even more important point here. They are forced to undergo plastic surgery so that they won't even recognize themselves."

Levent paused for a moment. Another bus passed by, and the urge to revolt raged as strongly as before.

"To what end?"

"Protection. The people in charge make sure that the people taken into the program have severed all ties with the past. All that's left is their appearance, and that's why plastic surgery is so important. Something like that might have happened to your friend as well. She was a dentist, right?"

Zahide had once been a dentist. And then a student, rushing from one ice-blue hallway at the university to the next.

"Yes, she was."

"And she graduated from an American university, didn't she?"

She did. But she cared little for ceremonies, and didn't attend the graduation event.

"Yes."

"So she knows English, which is something not so common for a traditional Muslim woman. She very well may have been destined for a stadium."

Zahide knew English. She had an accent, but was fluent. The thought of her being put through plastic surgery seven stories under a stadium was simply too much. How could she bear having her own face taken from her? No longer would light radiate from her eyes as she squinted when she smiled. Zahide was a woman of laughter, and the idea of anything being done to change that sent a chill through me.

"What!"

Another "what." Levent and I looked at each other. We were like a couple that had been together for years but were about to get into an argument in the middle of the street.

Breathlessly I said, "So you're saying that she may have been brainwashed and then forced to have plastic surgery?"

"That's what the Theta project is all about."

"But what's the point of it all?"

"It's for the future, Emel."

"Whose future?"

At that point Nadir touched my arm, warning me to keep calm. I nodded, vowing to do my best.

"It's all about the new order of the world. And it's also a way of reintegrating criminals into society."

"And I suppose you approve of this thing you call the new order?"

"I'm just trying to reassure you."

"Thank you!" I sneered. "You've really put me at ease."

At that point, Levent held his hands up as if to say that there was simply nothing he could do.

"How much money have you all made from this project, Levent?"

"Us?"

"You and your kind."

He smiles.

"We're professionals," he says, emphasizing the "we." But his voice betrayed a certain hesitation. I tried to soften my approach.

"Do you think it's really possible that Zahide may have part of the project?"

Levent smiled. Why would he smile? The thought crossed my mind that perhaps this man sitting across from me was some kind of lunatic.

"I don't know if your friend was ever taken into custody or not. In Istanbul, I worked for the witness protection program with people who were thought to be mentally unstable. But I don't know what the latest situation is."

"What do you think I should do now?"

I expected him to tell me to just keep calm and be patient. But then, in his accented English, he said:

"Emel, too much curiosity can be dangerous. You could be putting your life in danger. Enjoy your life, enjoy your time in DC."

His words were lost in the wind. Was it the wind of my thoughts? Outside, more buses went by. They all looked the same. The winter day seemed to whisper of spring, and for a moment I thought that I could hear people laughing in the distance. I could see traffic signs and the wall of the university campus, and the trees lining the street started going out of focus as disjointed memories began flashing through my mind. With those words, he was telling a young heroine who had set out on an adventure and vowed to cross all thresholds that she was no better than a Penelope destined to wait and watch as life passed her by. Or even worse, that Sohni would vanish beneath the water, never to be seen again. I was that miserable heroine who refused to turn back and clung to my search for freedom in life. That was the source of my dignity, and no matter how bedraggled it may be, it was all I had. At least that's what I believed. Everyone believes in something. Some people want to save the world, and others may simply go off in search of battles with windmills. But I had made my choice; I would be that heroine, and continue in my search for Zahide, clinging to my hope that I would find her. I knew the beginning of the story, and I had a right to know the end. Didn't I? Had I deluded myself? I was going to find Zahide, there was no way around it. And I had a feeling that when I did, everything would get better.

His admonition to just enjoy my life and shake off my curiosity was preposterous at best.

I decided to stop hanging on his every word and treat what he said as nothing more than a script that had been hastily dashed off. But it wasn't exactly his words that seemed twisted and incoherent. It was the script in my own mind that was jumbled and confused.

Levent had the last word. Professionals always do. Stop thinking. Enjoy your life.

Just like the meaning of his name, Levent was bold and forceful.

As I tried to understand Zahide, just who she was, I was shaken by an arbitrariness that constantly welled up inside me and was steadily choking off my breath. It wasn't anger or despair at all, but something altogether different, something that pulled everything into itself while nullifying it all at the same time. I felt as though I would be constantly driven back, defeated because I had no one in my life; I, too, was a stray and would pay the price for that sense of not belonging. I was forever caught up in a net of feeling that everything was both so familiar and strange at the same time, a feeling interwoven with sadness that brimmed with laughter. Perhaps that's how I seemed to Levent and all those like him. He was complacent, untroubled. Even their concerns were complacent. Still, I thought, I shouldn't be unfair. It wasn't that people like him were untroubled; they were unscathed by trouble. Levent represented my defeat before the world, before death. That was something he would never understand, that I was a Zahide myself, and I had to be wary of the notion that the researcher is actually part of the research itself. The contradictions I carried within were simply beyond him. His kind of people merely give humanistic responses, appropriate and sound predictions, and nothing more.

"I understand you," he said.

That was the last thing he should have said.

I was completely thrown off. For a moment, I'd been on the verge of opening myself up and revealing everything about that web of fate I found myself trapped in to the one person who perhaps could be my undoing. In a way, it was like the love that prisoners sometimes feel for their executioners. I knew I was exaggerating, but the ball of thread had already unraveled. Would Levent say anything else? Of course he would. That's what his kind do.

For instance he might talk about his youth and how he too joined in protests and sit-ins against the government. He might talk about the fact that he is against terrorism and all that he has done in the struggle to prevent it. Or perhaps he would say that he was in fact a good person whose heart was in the right place.

But that wouldn't be enough for me. I felt like I was trapped in a hopeless dilemma, on the verge of giving myself over to the whims of time. But my desire to know more, to know the truth, couldn't be silenced so easily. I knew that, even though it may not have been based on objective reasons or a clear stance on terrorism, or friendships and humanity. And all at once, a sentiment that I had been carrying inside for years burst forth:

"There is a void within me that you cannot fill, no matter how much you think you know. Arrogance should know that it has its own limits!"

I thought that was all, but I surprised even myself by what I said next in reply to Levent, who turned to me and said, "Emel, that's a rather audacious thing to say, and if you will pardon me, dangerously verging on schizophrenic."

Schizophrenic. That word touched a nerve: "That may be so, but at least I have the courage to stand up and speak my mind!"

But I should have realized that Levent was merely functional for me. Through him, I was supposed to see that Zahide was none other than that which was missing within me. At any other time, I would have delved into theories about that void I carried inside, trying to weave it together with political facts. But at that moment, nothing could have been further from my thoughts. I was what I was. My curiosity about Zahide may have had little to do with me as a person in that void, but for the first time, even if there was a feeling of emptiness, I felt I belonged somewhere. As Levent's voice grew ever more distant, I set about observing myself, almost to the point of narcissism.

That void proved to be far less problematic than I expected. It was rather like breaking an egg, or noticing a run in your pantyhose before you walk outside. And at that moment, I felt something I'd never felt before. At the same time, a desire to live and a desire to die called out, and I felt it physically like a scratch in my throat. I was nearing that final point where curiosity thrives on the making of mistakes, and I recalled Levent's warning: Don't be too curious!

It was like the feeling you get when you ask the wrong questions at the wrong time. But we are always driven to find the right beliefs, make the right decisions, find our way with the right words, stay focused on the right energy, formulate the right opinions, stay on the right points. But no matter how I tried to deny it, I was spurred on by a thirst to know more. Heroes set out buoyed by hope and perseverance, and without curiosity we would never arrive at the truth. At the same time, it was driving me into that void, to Zahide.

Struggling in Nadir's arms, at last I managed to break free and started to run. And how I ran! Perhaps he called out to me, or maybe everyone was simply too stunned to say anything at all. But it didn't matter, because I was in no state to put up with questions.

I rushed headlong down the university's main boulevard as though

I would plunge into the Potomac River, and the stores whizzed past left and right.

I ran as though I were water trying to find its course, sluicing through mud. At times I slithered like a black snake, and one moment I was Emel and the next moment I was Zahide.

With each step, I drew closer. To what? It didn't matter, I just needed to keep going forward. But at one point, I stopped. Something stopped me. I glanced around, my mouth creased in a tight line. I caught the scent of onions, and realized I was in front of a diner. Then I looked across the street and saw that there was a large secondhand store. The name of the store was "Underground."

Just as I was about to dash towards the door, someone reached out and stopped me in the middle of the street. "If you wander away from home, you'll fall prey to wolves," I heard a voice say.

Indeed, I had fallen prey.

13

Home? Did you say home? What does home mean to me, Zahide Sohni Mühür? My home is this stadium. In the past? That house in Kensington wasn't home for me, Levent Bey. I've been telling you that for some time. I'm sure you must understand that by now. I'm changing. My body is changing, just like my soul. My hands are changing, just like the destiny they grasp.

Listen:

Sometimes, I'd call out to the walls, saying "Zahide." That went on for a long while. In the end, that house became nothing more than a black pit, draining away my energy. And the fact that I couldn't focus on anything made me wary of the world.

I was guilty.

But still, I needed friendship. Even in this foreign land I needed it.

How did I find out I was guilty?

My neighbor Leyla. That's what she said: "Friendship is truly essential." I took her at her word. She was Iranian, and a warm, sincere woman. When she invited me over for tea so I could meet some of her friends, I couldn't say no. My loneliness weighed upon me in those days.

She said friendship was essential. But once I had Emel in my life. And there's the one who wears the ghost uniform, but all he did was dull my mind with injections, and everything would turn into a void.

He took me to the underground land of the dead and they spoke with us. We passed through gates. Seven. Each time I passed through one, part of me would be left behind. Then I'd be reunited with the dead, my dead. The man in the ghost uniform said: If you want to see your dead, you have to confess your crimes.

I was guilty.

The man in the ghost uniform beat me. I knew that he was, in fact, Richard.

Sometimes he raped me as well.

But I was guilty.

Admit your guilt and I'll take you to the underground world, the man in the ghost uniform said. He'd read my mind.

In the land of the dead, everyone was alive. My mother, my father, my brother, my oldest son Ahmet, İzzet . . .

And Emel was there. I was surprised to see her. She was dead.

The man in the ghost uniform told me everything. Emel had died in an earthquake along with her family. I wept again and again.

Because friendship is essential.

Leyla, my neighbor, said that.

In my house surrounded by trees, I longed for weeks to see another human face. "Sure," I said to Leyla, "I'll come if nothing comes up." Then I added, "But I won't be able to stay for long."

No one ever visits me. Except for the man in the ghost uniform.

My thoughts always turn to the divine task I have been charged with carrying out.

Who am I?

I used to be a sleeper terrorist. It was I who should have been the most harshly condemned. But now, in the name of the future, I have been given a divine task. A new world order.

For a long time I haven't received any messages.

But I sense that there are hidden messages everywhere.

In the morning I'd sit on my porch and think about my crime. Do I still?

Yes.

We live in a stadium, seven floors underground. I have a house that resembles the one in Kensington. I even have a yard, and neighbors. I have Leyla. I even have the man in the ghost uniform. I go to my neighbor's for tea.

I live with the dead seven floors underground. The future is ours. We'll build the future. We'll eradicate crime from the face of the earth without scaring a soul. Those ordinary minds will be untouched by fear. The reality of the world is already too much for them.

Why?

Because friendship is essential, and every message is critical.

That's why I perceived my neighbor Leyla's invitation as a message. Clearly, some new developments had taken place on the team, and the best way to let me know about them was a tea party.

But the messages weren't limited to that. I heard some strange sounds one morning. For a moment, I thought the house was surrounded. In such cases, the best thing to do is to keep calm, so I grabbed my air rifle and took up position. The sounds kept getting closer. Closer and closer. It was as if the pile of leaves in the garden had been taken over by unknown forces, a harbinger of death for me and my sons. Just as I was about to pull the trigger, I saw something that looked like a carved wooden figure and that's why I thought death was upon me. It became broader and longer, and the carved wooden figure turned into a head with shifting eyes. Then I realized it was a group of deer foraging for food. The sound of the deer woke up my sons, and they went out into the yard and starting playing with them. It wasn't the fault of the deer, and I don't blame them. But my sons went off with them. They'll be back the next morning, I said to myself. They didn't come back. The boys went with the deer and never came back.

Messages are critical. Friendship is essential.

Here's how I remember what happened after the deer incident. I waited a while. A few days, a few weeks. The boys didn't come back. I realized that it must be a message. Then I told the man in the ghost uniform, "I'm ready, take me underground." So he took me on a long journey. Then we came to the stadium.

I met people I knew along the way. It was a pleasant journey. Messages are important. Friendship is essential, Levent Bey. You know, friendship is essential.

How did I meet the man in the ghost uniform? Him? He never hurts anyone. He's my husband.

He's my neighbor and an important person in my life. He's a prophet. He's my family.

Messages are very important. Leyla's tea party is very important. The message is clear: It is time to take action.

Everything grew old and left with the deer, Levent Bey. All that's left behind is an empty house. According to the man in the ghost uniform, some things were telling me to be ready. Some things. Who knows, maybe receivers had been implanted in the deer, or maybe they were FBI agents disguised as deer. Maybe they were on our side; it was my fault, they were checking to see if I was carrying out my task. Oh, those deer! I began reporting what was happening around me. But they've never stopped following me. They come and visit me in my home under the stadium. They come to my yard. I have an incredible yard seven floors underground. I have neighbors. I go to tea parties every day. We chat. The deer come. I ask the deer about my sons. They're fine, they say.

The man in the ghost uniform confuses me. There's no two ways about it; he's a bastard through and through. One day I'll grab him by the collar and throw him out into the yard. I'll bury him under the trees. Then, and only then, I'll go and beg the deer to give me back my sons. I was guilty. I was a sleeper terrorist, but now I'm ready to save the world, I'll tell them. I'll say friendship is essential, messages are very important. If you're my friends, come over for tea one day. I'll invite them to my porch. I have a large ghara. Do you know what a ghara is? A washtub made of fired clay. I use it as a coffee table on my porch. Sometimes, the man in the ghost uniform hides there, thinking that he'll frighten me. Idiot. Who the hell are you to scare me?

Leyla's house is directly opposite my house in the stadium, just like it was in Kensington. Every day, we chat; every day we laugh.

But I'm suspicious of Leyla. Every day, she invites me over for tea. And the man in the ghost uniform warns me every day. Supposedly, he inseminates me every day. I am barren. After he rapes me, I grab him, throw him in the ghara, and choke him again and again and again.

I'm suspicious of everyone.

But there's one thing that I can't cast from my thoughts. The dead I saw underground and the essence of friendship. And the masks.

Masks?

Before we entered the stadium, the man in the ghost uniform told me as we were passing through the last gate that they'd give me a real mask and that I would put it on. "We think Emel's mask would fit you the best." I didn't understand. "Emel's mask," he said. I saw Emel as I passed through the fifth gate. She was alive when she was pulled from the rubble. Then she bled to death. I agreed to put Emel's mask on.

Next time, if there's ever a next time, Levent Bey, don't be surprised to see me as someone else. But there won't be a next time.

14

Yet there was a next time. The surgery was delayed, and she was oppo-site me as her usual self.

Again she was the one narrating the story. The weary narrator.

Had it not been for the peculiarities she experienced with the deer and the phone call the day before, Zahide would not have lifted a finger and would have quietly continued to play the role that had been cast for her. But since those events happened and there were questions to be asked, she didn't really have a choice. I'm ready now, she said to the man in the ghost uniform. He was Richard the neighbor. Richard wanted Zahide to call him "the man in the ghost uniform" and insisted on calling Zahide "Sohni."

That day Zahide took it upon herself to wait, her eyes puffed up from crying since the boys had left. According to what the man in the ghost uniform said, it was now time to play a game because that was the only way they could make the trip to the land of the dead. The man in the ghost uniform said that people who don't go to the land of the dead don't appreciate the value of life. At least that night, Zahide had to go with him. But it was impossible to squeeze all the friendship, hatred and secrets in the world into one night; she should know that.

As the man in the ghost uniform had said, they would descend under-ground. They would go through the seven gates of the underground.

They had to leave behind a talisman at each gate in order so that Zahide could pass through. Otherwise, the land of the dead would remain a dream. But the man in the ghost uniform passed through the gates without a talisman. He was cloaked in a kind of armor that brought together all the mortality and immortality in his soul and made all the pain vanish.

Underground. Easier said than done!

On the evening after she had lost her sons, Zahide knew that she had to flow down the drain of the bathtub upstairs and find a way to join the flow of the city water.

But the pipe was blocked.

"Sometimes the best way to deal with a blocked pipe is pressure," the man in the ghost uniform said. He told her that sometimes we have to tolerate—to a certain extent—people who make their living by pursuing the memories and mistakes that become entangled in our lives.

Pressure and the revenge that it inspires. Those were concepts Zahide had come to know quite well in the last five years. Unable to bear her husband's cruelty, she had fled, meaning that such a flood of light could wash over the life of anyone who was oppressed. But that wasn't all. Zahide had been included in the organization in a way that she never expected. Perhaps she herself had even desired that. Wasn't youth about getting through all the difficult times and persevering? The innocent young soldiers of the Pakistani Ziya-ul-Hak, who were behind the forces that took her parents from her one morning, weren't the only source of suffering. When the government asserted itself as the wellspring of power, it said so with a certain firmness, and that same firmness had kept her right beside her husband, it enveloped her body, invading her dreams across every century. She was never directly involved in any major operations, of course, but she did work with people who were close to the lower ranks to ensure the security of the members of the organization and she collected funds and issued fake invoices. Her husband, a doctor, held a high position in the organization, and he knew almost everything that happened. In the beginning, it seemed like everything was fine. Revenge would come by force and, no matter how strange it may be to say, not once did they ever think of abandoning the human spirit.

Perhaps that's why when Zahide woke up one morning, she realized that her hands were covered in blood. Actually she was pregnant with her third child and was miscarrying. But it seemed to her that the blood on her hands wasn't just from the fetus inside her but was the blood of the world's beating heart; her body would merge with the world and the bleeding wouldn't stop, it would never stop. The world was heading towards a blood bath, a sea of blood.

Force and pressure. The blood wouldn't clot. It was strange, the blood would never clot and Zahide would swim in a river of blood, flowing away from herself, her fetus and the world. It was almost like a joke in bad taste; in the song "Sohni Remembered," the lyrics read, "If the waters suddenly turn red, you should know, Sohni, you're swimming in the wrong place."

Someone trying to get to the other side of the river would think of something like that. Zahide was probably swimming in the wrong place!

Zahide took her two sons and sought refuge in the witness protection program, an ordeal that would last for months.

She fled from her husband. Months later, she found herself cowering in that house hidden among trees in Kensington, Maryland. She took refuge and began to wait.

She didn't die.

But she waited.

She waited until she forgot what she was waiting for, hoping that whatever came by force would leave by force. She had hope.

But it didn't leave, and she waited.

Then she got a phone call. She panicked, because her phone had been blocked, just like her soul. It was her brother, an old member of the organization. "How'd you find this number?" Zahide asked, her voice trembling. "I need to see you," her brother said. She agreed. "But just so you know, I'm in some kind of land of the dead," he said and hung up in fear.

The telephone call seemed to seep into every corner the night, filling it, and the voice of her brother echoed in Zahide's ears. Whenever she heard a noise, she shuddered; when the wind blew, she prayed to God. The pressure had been set loose and howled inside that house surrounded by large trees.

She felt the pressure. It was her brother's voice:

You're in danger.

It was her brother's unease.

It was her brother's voice laden with judgment:

You're in the wrong place.

She felt the pressure:

It was that which hummed and murmured.

Towards dawn, there was so much pressure that the water main in front of the house burst. Then the deer came.

It seemed like the water was trying to be a monsoon shower and make the street disappear beneath it. Zahide was confused.

A sound emerged from Zahide's heart and moved up her throat, but it pulled back as soon as it touched the air.

Then it happened; the deer came. The FBI and many more. What beguiled her were the pieces broken off from dreams that were timeless and placeless. There was no point in confronting such memories; Zahide merely wanted to live in the present. She thought that way because she wanted to see the city as a kind of makeshift bride rather than seeing herself as a patch stitched onto the city. Everything was new, but not in her eyes; she was centuries old, exhausted. What's new was Maryland, seeing it for the first time, trying to understand it, mentally mapping it, nurturing it, trying to work it out. That was the wonderful part. The changing of places. The wonderful part was slipping out of the roles that were cast for you and turning your luck around. For the first time since she arrived in Maryland, she was able to find peace after all those nightmares. She felt for the first time that she was dying. And it all seemed like a game. Where had she played that game? Just then she was walking along Chance Avenue. At the last moment, she saw a left turn sign pointing to Time Boulevard.

Was that the real face of Maryland?

Once again she became confused. Then she saw another sign: "Go straight on Chance Avenue to reach Time Boulevard." Just like in *Alice in Wonderland*, she thought. With just one turn, she'd be back on a straight road. She needed time to grasp that Time Boulevard was pregnant with every road there is, leading every which way, and Zahide was a traveler destined to use up time. Zahide thought she was dead.

At that moment, she made a sudden turn.

It happened.

It happened, but she noticed the flickering lights behind her. Red, white, blue, accompanied by the sounds of sirens. They were coming after her. All around was that light, all around was the sound of sirens. They were all in front of her house in Kensington. She was caught.

According to the witnesses who were lined up along the road, they put Zahide and two corpses into a car.

Zahide isn't rational.

Zahide isn't level-headed.

Her heart of the East was too embittered to think that comprehending life is only possible through a logical reconciliation of her experiences and herself at that point in time. That's how it was, even though she knew that belonging was a hindrance. That's how it was, even though she knew that being from the East caused her the most pain as a woman. In short, the story of her own life was too complicated to be bogged down by the rules and regulations of that large country. And it was not side effects but Zahide herself who made things that way. Perhaps she was a sleeper terrorist in the eyes of those people; perhaps she should've mentioned that she had a brother in the land of the dead. She should've said she was innocent. But it was too late. She should've said that terrorism brought suspicion against hundreds of thousands of innocent Muslims in the wake of all those people who died and that Muslims could not be blamed for it all. No natural power in the world was capable of that. Yet Zahide knew she wasn't innocent herself; her hands were covered in blood. But whose hands aren't bloody?

Everyone's hands were covered in blood.

Except for the police in front of the house. They believed they were pure and would save the world.

Ambition is like that. Faith is like that. The officers shot fiery glances at Zahide's half-dead eyes.

"Looks like suicide. The children are dead, the woman's sure of it," someone said. Zahide heard but couldn't answer.

At that moment Zahide truly wished she were a suicide bomber ready to detonate herself. It was the first time she ever thought that. She wanted to detonate herself in the face of the power that had come crashing down over her, to spite the piqued desperation of the police and FBI agents who had gathered in front of the house, to snap her revolt up and down the street like a whip, rising up against that damned blessed officer in the line of duty, against the creases in the corner of his eyes when he smiled, against the way his freckles made his expressions all so human.

For some reason, Zahide pictured that bomb not as a weapon that claimed lives but something that would stun them with a powerful stench, and she relished the idea of such a device that would choke those officers of the law, even though she might be sent to prison. At one point, she glanced at her hands and saw that the blood-red had faded to pink.

The police stood on the street as though they were the sole rulers of the world, maintaining law and order.

There was no need to maintain law and order, she thought.

Zahide grinned hysterically. She had to get up from the stretcher and find a telephone booth.

But finding a telephone booth would be as difficult as coaxing an angel down from heaven. A simple phone booth, that was all she wanted, despite the fact that she was even too tired to say, "Life is a miracle." Even if she could call someone, she knew no one would answer. The only thought that could console her would be, "I don't know anyone in this city." She felt the weight of Maryland pressing down upon her. How long had she been from Maryland? No, that wasn't the right question. How long has she been without Maryland? At her home, with her trees. Maryland? Was she from Maryland enough to say Mary-what? Is that the name of a new drug? She was part of Maryland enough to say that it wasn't far from DC, but too far from herself. She somehow remembered its size, surface area, subway stations and parks, but only as much as she'd remember an aging friend from high school or someone she'd just met yesterday. Maryland was like the blurry outline of someone that Zahide didn't know and didn't care to know anything about. Nothing more.

Zahide thought to herself, "I'm dead." Still, isn't it she who's talking? I put my sons to bed, I turned the gas on, and we all died together.

"What if I'm not dead? I don't know anyone in this city."

Time rushed by.

"If I'm not dead, I surely don't know anyone here."

She didn't give up; she wasn't going to give up.

"I must have some . . . acquaintances."

She said the letters of the alphabet, A, B, C, all the way up to H. Then she went from H to K, tracing a soft dip. Then found herself in a gouged out hollow. P.

Then came R.

The sky took shape.

R, in all its exuberance.

And Sohni remembered:

Richard.

Her neighbor.

She'd remember.

And Sohni remembered . . .

That's how the song began.

She drifted off and retraced her story all the way back to the beginning.

Dear esteemed . . . Listen. You listen, too, Levent Koryürek. And you, Müge İplikçi. You use me too, like everyone else.

A woman with two children comes to Kensington under the FBI's witness protection program. She was kept waiting for nearly five hours at Dulles Airport.

She comes to an empty house. There are two blankets, one bed and a fold-out sofa. The kitchen, on the other hand, is fully equipped. Oven, pots and pans, glasses, toaster, coffee maker. They take refuge on the sofa bed and sleep. They wake up in the morning and find that the house is full of bamboo plants. Bamboo is everywhere.

There's no Richard.

Richard isn't there the next day, either.

The following day?

A week later?

Just then, a knock at the door.

It's Richard and Shaena. A bottle in Shaena's hand. She says, "It's our custom to give some of our homemade punch to the newcomers." Later Zahide drinks some of the punch. The more she drinks, the more differently she sees the world. Is it an alcoholic drink? she wonders. She can't be sure, but after a certain point, it doesn't matter. Her mind vanishes.

In all senses, Richard doesn't exist there.

Time passes by.

Then one day Richard shows up. Not through the door but through the bamboo plants. From among the bamboo plants between their houses, with three bamboo shoots in his hand.

Richard is quite enthusiastic about the bamboo shoots. He says that they're delicious when grilled. "I learned it from a Chinese friend; if you sprinkle some black pepper on them, they're amazing. Do you have an oven? Yes? Come on, let's cook them." They cook the bamboo shoots. The smell of seaweed—which for some reason means Pakistan for Zahide—and smoked meat—which reminds Richard of his child-hood—fills the house.

Black pepper is sprinkled over the bamboo shoots. They eat together on the porch. They do everything in silence. The bamboo shoots are all eaten. The wind blows through the the bamboo surrounding the porch. Then they start talking about life.

Richard starts the conversation. He says he works at the *Washington Post*. Shaena? She's a civil servant, retired from the military. He asks Zahide not to inquire about the details. Zahide understands; she doesn't insist. You can't actually call me a journalist. Mine is, how should I put it, a somewhat strange job. It requires a bit of a special ability. Ability? Yes, I have an ability. What's that? Now, it'll sound strange to you. No, it won't. Well, I can tell when people are going to die. I don't believe it. Don't. Really? Really. How so? I don't know, I just can. Is it an innate ability? I'm not really sure. When did you find out? When I was a teenager. We had a neighbor. He had a son, named Luke. I was fourteen at the time, and he was twelve. That morning he said good morning to me. I looked at Luke's face. He had a dimpled smile. Then something happened. You know, people sense when they're going to die; I guess he gave me that sort of a signal. He said, I'm going to die today, Richard. It was a strange, metallic kind of murmur. I asked him what the hell he was talking about. He looked at me and said he hadn't said anything. And Luke died that day. Then? I became obsessed with Luke afterwards. His dreams started coming into mine. My past, his past. I couldn't eat or sleep because of the trembling. Then . . . Well, this will sound even more incredible. One night Luke called out to me to join him. You're in a lot of pain, Richard. You should come and see this place, he said. Where are you talking about? I asked. More or less I knew. This is the underground, Luke said. The realm of the dead. You can't even imagine what it's like. You should come and see it for yourself. But I can't go there, Luke, I said. I'm a mortal. I knew most of the legends about the underground. Of course, Luke knew that, too. It's not like you think, Richard, you're different. How am I different? I asked. I can't tell, but you don't need a talisman, he told me. And that night, with Luke's help, I made my first trip to the realm of the dead. And then I woke up. The trembling was over. I knew I could be with people when they'd perished and there was nothing to be afraid of.

On the porch surrounded by bamboo, Richard told Zahide that he could take her to the realm of the dead. Why me? asked Zahide. Death has sunk into your eyes, Richard said: It's obvious that you miss some people who passed away far before it was their time.

Now I have to find Richard, Zahide thought. Now's the time.

Was that Richard?

It wasn't exactly like that or unlike that.

One day, he came and sat opposite me in his military uniform.

How do I look? he asked.

Zahide told him he looked dreadful.

This uniform was my father's, he said.

Richard, for God's sake that's an SS uniform, Zahide said.

Correct. My father was a Nazi officer, Richard said.

Then he went too far. He said:

I killed him. I poisoned him. Everyone thought his experiments were the end of him, but I poisoned him with my own hands.

He looked drunk. He always looked drunk.

What are you saying, Richard, Zahide asked. Aren't you afraid of me? Aren't you afraid I will tell someone?

Then he became even stranger, and began making odd sounds.

Why should I be afraid? You don't exist! You're a wall. You're not alive!

Richard must have lost his mind.

Zahide lost her patience.

What are you talking about? How do you know who I am? You can't know my past and future. I'm just an ordinary woman living here with her two children, keeping to herself. Do you even know what kind of a bind I'm in? I must be out of my mind spending time with a lunatic like you.

The man opposite her was the same crazed person.

I know who you are. I know you.

Who? Who am I, then? Tell me. Who am I?

Haha, you're a fugitive. You're the FBI's bitch. You're a Pakistani whore. An Al-Qaeda militant. I know all your secrets. You're supposedly under witness protection, but we're the ones actually protecting you, me and my sister. Who do you think this house belongs to? They're going to finish you off. Do you think sluts like you live forever? Look around, do you see any communists? The United States is a holy land, and you and your like should know that. You're all bitches and together with your bastards you're bringing the world to ruin. My country is an empire, just so you know. We're going to chop off all of your heads. We're going to annihilate you.

Is that Richard?

Maybe.

I must find Richard, Zahide thinks as she's being wheeled out of the house on a stretcher.

That's the Richard that Zahide kicked off the porch. Whether he's the real one or not is hard to tell. But that's the next memory. The Richard in the letter R that occurs to Zahide has not yet spilled the secrets in her subconscious; he hasn't told Zahide about herself in such a brutally clear way. Still, a few days later he'd come and apologize to Zahide, leaving a bouquet of chrysanthemums on the side table on the porch with a card that read "At least for the sake of the realm of the dead." But it was vain. Zahide's heart will already have been broken. And afterwards, the rendition program will bring everything to an end.

Yes, that's a different episode. The Richard in Zahide's mind is the mysterious prince of the realm of the dead. Not that lunatic man of the earth, the victim of a manic-depressive father.

The Richard in Zahide's R is a likeable Richard. Someone she knows will run to help her as soon as she dials the phone. That R is not the victim of an experiment. He's a journalist who writes a column in the obituary section of the *Washington Post*. A man with a special ability that he acquired when he was fourteen years old. He's not the kind of person who would resurrect the Theta Project in his father's formulas with his punch. Zahide's R is a good person.

Zahide wants to talk to that good Richard. If only you knew what happened to me, she wants to say to him. I need your help, please come, she wants to say.

The sirens and the lights continue. So does the din of the police radio.

In Zahide's mind, Richard isn't the kind of person who goes through life in pursuit of mistakes; he accepts life as it is. He is the R of the likeable Richard. He's the Richard who would tell Zahide that "the best solution is to become one with the city water system so you can reach everyone, and you might even scare some people and please others. You'll be invisible as you explore the underground world."

Zahide is aware that she has no choice but to listen to Richard.

"Get me out of this bind, take me with you," she murmurs on the stretcher.

"Richard, save me. Take me to the underground, Richard."

* * *

That was the night when everything was proven. Zahide had to flow out of a tiny crack of the bathtub upstairs and somehow find a way down the front of the house to become one with the city water.

That night, within inches of her goal, we see Richard in a state that resembles drinking water. Speaking the language of people who share the same fate, we begin to flow towards revenge, towards the past and future. Except for Richard's occasional tirades, it could even be considered an amusing journey. He's quite beside himself; he casts me as Ishtar in this journey. I don't mind; frankly it suits me to play the role of the unfortunate goddess looking for her sister. We look for my sister for seven nights.

Towards the end, Richard's voice becomes the voice of the realm of the dead: You now have crossed over a magical threshold into the realm of the dead, Zahide. You should know that means crossing into the land of rebirth. You're a true hero now. From now on, you'll have two lives. One in which you journey to the underground, and the other on earth. I can't say that one is more real than the other, or that one is less of a dream. You can call one a myth, and the other real life. You can call one the things you run away from, and the other the things that you're caught up by. From now on, it'll all be the same for you. Perhaps the reality and the dream will be so much alike that you won't be able to tell them apart. Is that the enlightenment of the dead? You won't even be able to know what's real and what's a dream.

"Are you ready to see all the dead in your life, Zahide?" Richard asks, gazing intently at the woman on the stretcher. "Do you accept me as the prince of darkness of your dreams?"

Zahide answers neither yes nor no. She thinks that all the oppressed people in the world would do the same.

15

It's late. The surgery is delayed again.

I preferred to tell this part in Sohni's own voice. Tomorrow, I'm going back to DC, trying to forget the wreckage I'm leaving behind. Her Mount Qaf, the nightmare of us all and the shame of humanity. God damn it all, but that's what happened.

The night gleamed in all its splendor. No, the night wasn't gleaming. The iron stakes plunged into the ground in the stadium were gleaming just like the steel posts that soared upwards. In the early quiet of night, the meaning ascribed to that structure with bright colorful light bulbs was nothing but the alluring stadium itself. The grand impression that dark edifice created on us mortal beings was, supposedly, the truest tale of all. Mount Qaf Stadium was the pure white moon of the night, a glorious glimmer, a colossal festivity.

The moral of the story is simple: That night was the best news that massive solemn heap of iron could ever promise. The Grand Derby.

Everyone knew their place: the amusing omnipresent reporters, the short-tempered football players, the madly cheering fans, the steam rising with the scent of grilled meat, haggard police, lurching traffic, the shadows of self-confident men, the shadows that left behind less ash, people with painted faces, the arrogant, the plain local residents, rhythmical cheerleaders, soft drink vendors with or without permits. They all

knew their roles. From the plastic shields of the police to the delicate glimmer of minarets on the opposite shore, from the fresh grass of the stadium to the rough and rowdy people in the parking lot, they were all there, everyone who was alive in all their emotions, which should come as no surprise. But at the same time, there was such resignation; souls gave themselves up for others, scattering their jumbled memories. And then the announcement was made, the lead-in to the main event:

"Dear spectators, the grand gathering at Mount Qaf Stadium is about to begin."

* * *

According to the man in the ghost uniform, it wasn't actually a house but a cramped cell in the basement of a stadium, nothing more, and I was a helpless shadow who had lost herself, lost her past and present. Everything I saw was but a reflection from a magic lantern of my past and had nothing to do with the present moment, in which I was a mere puppet. For him I was a slave in eternal captivity, much like himself.

It is simply too much to bear.

In my house surrounded by trees, I'd longed for months to see another human face. If I could write it, that would be my real story, and I suppose that was also the root of my problems. Had it not been for that man in the strange uniform who gave me, and probably the walls, advice every once in a while, perhaps everything could have flowed in some sort of turquoise calm. But my situation with the man in the ghost uniform was hopeless. I don't know exactly who or what he was. He would say that was further proof that I had lost myself. Just keeping myself alive was causing my mind to plunge deeper into a somnolent state of numbness. And it seemed like all those dreams were a natural part of the process. That's what he would haughtily say. Every five or ten days, he'd show up at the house, either as himself or a vision of him would flicker on the wall, and then he'd go away. I doubt he had anything to do with my real life. Not that I had one, as far as he was concerned. Luckily for me he was just a shadow, so I didn't have to take him seriously. He was a destitute wretch of a being, so for a long time I kept silent. The extent of our relationship was obvious: I was just a stopping point and he was a shadow with an uncertain heart who came and went. We went on like this for a long time.

But one day that untarnished relationship came to an end. I ended it all. It had simply become unbearable. He blamed me for what I was going through and said that I needed to keep my mind sharp. He became a seer, constantly giving me advice.

No, I said. Enough.

When I turned the man in the ghost uniform into a scarecrow and tossed him into the yard, silvery leaves were falling from the large syca-more tree. The leaves fell in waves, covering the ground and leaving no trace of the scarecrow.

That was how I felt at first, but then my relief was transformed into guilt.

That's why I felt so lonely afterwards. It may seem odd, but loneli-ness can drive you to do things that you later regret even though you were right in your own way. That's why I resented the leaves, and swore at the season and my choices. There was nothing to do. I was alone, and winter was looming on the horizon.

I realized that missing someone can be so meaningful, even if that person was nothing a ghost. I tried everything, but gloom filled the house and billowed out into the yard.

I gave in.

To fate?

No, of course not. Heroes don't give in to fate.

During our last conversation on the porch, the man in the ghost uniform and I talked about that and discussed heroes and surrender. The man in the ghost uniform with the epaulettes which I found so charming dared give me advice and pontificated on civilizations' principles of existence and destruction and went on to drone about the lack of choices between the past and the present. His face like a blank mask, he said that only birth could get the better of death.

When he spoke those words and vowed that holy virtues were no longer relevant, he had the bearing of someone who was still living. He argued that the idea of peace, as with all wars, was the product of a devious mind. Change, he claimed, was just a meaningless six-letter word, and he said that the idea of seizing eternity when the world was in such a hopeless state was an empty dream. But still, there was hope. Only the idea of rebirth could circumvent the end, and for that we had to be shattered into pieces.

Only a ghost could say such a thing.

As time went by I noticed that his old torn uniform had become even more threadbare in the howling wind that first knocked down the pink geraniums and then the bamboo plants behind us.

It was clear that he'd been through many wars and seen much destruction.

It was clear that he'd seen many periods of peace following that destruction.

Despite that, he talked about what it means to shatter into pieces and the state of eternal being that could follow. It was sheer nonsense.

"You're a corpse," I shouted. "Why do I even listen to you?"

He said nothing.

Maybe that's why I drove home the point.

"I've had it with you," I said. "You don't understand what I'm going through. You don't understand the times. You don't care about plans of escape. You just sit there in your ragged uniform and lay down the law, but I can't even see your face. You get into my dreams and twist them around."

In the end, I had no choice but to say, "Get the hell away from me!"

But he did nothing.

He was nothing but a dishonorable brute.

"Don't," he whined. My God, was he crying? That was simply too much. I wondered, what had I done to deserve this? And he sat there, a pathetic creature.

"Enough of the crying," I said. "I have no patience for it. I can't stand people who don't understand struggle or stand up for themselves." I kept raising my voice. Sitting up in my chair, I shouted, "Because living means resisting."

A deathly silence fell over the porch.

"There were times when I was honorable and dignified," he said.

"Then what about the state you're in right now?" I said.

"I've seen many kings and slaves," he said quietly. "All the magic."

"No, I don't want your foolish ideas," I said. "I'm talking about changing the world, and look at what you're saying!"

"You can't change the world as it is now. Especially like this," he added.

"You're pathetic," I yelled. I was starting to lose control.

"I've seen it all," he said.

"Good for you!" I said. "In your account, heroes have never existed in the world, which you say hasn't changed and can't change."

"But in the modern . . ."

His persistence was exasperating.

"For heaven's sake! Enough with that already!" I snapped.

He wept softly, trembling.

That's when I dragged him out to the backyard. I pulled him in his uniform through the dirt and, unable to resist, spat on him.

He was still crying and mumbling:

"After all that torture, they buried me in snow, in heaps of souls. They raped me, they killed me. Modern man is dead. The hero has ceased to be as a modern man. Modernity has killed the hero and men. But I couldn't truly die."

I piled more and more leaves onto the void of his face and screamed, "Die this time!" The more I screamed, the more vehement I became. But it wasn't enough to stop that corpse from saying one more thing:

Per me si va tra la Perduta Gente Sohni.

Per me si va tra . . .

And then he said something else, which I actually could understand:

"The way among lost souls runs through me, Sohni. It is up to me when the time comes to revive lost people and those who bid farewell to life, and I fill their minds with memories and recreate their pasts."

* * *

Zahide paused at that moment and turned to me and said something. She didn't want me to tape this bit, but I recorded it anyway:

"Levent, dear Levent, one day, I'm going to kill Richard. He was the one who interfered in my life, and once and for all I want his prying fingers out of my life. Promise you'll be there with me when that day comes."

I could say neither yes nor no. That's what any honorable scholar would have done.

16

Richard. It was his hand that grabbed my shoulder in the middle of the street.

At the moment, that was the last thing I needed. His face was pale and he looked upset.

"Hello, Emel."

I looked at him. He was like a lifeless shadow. The spindly branches of the Judas trees around the Potomac River were swaying in the wind. Richard didn't say anything else.

"They call this place the Underground," I stammered.

"Yes," Richard said. "I suppose they mean that have everything. Let's go inside. You'll see what I mean."

* * *

I'd dreamt about that moment when I had to choose between the door and the street. Even when we are left without a choice, we still make a decision. Breathlessly running from what Levent had told me, I found myself face to face with Richard and his strangely sticky, ghostly way of acting threw me off. Had I led myself to such an inevitable point? I still had a choice; I didn't have to go inside. And regardless of what happened, I may have remained blind to what destiny awaited me.

But Richard's sincerity seemed almost palpable. Despite his fatigue, he still exuded a certain energy. Like a hero, he opened the door for me and gestured for me to go inside. I went in, not because he held some irresistible charm over me, but because I felt drawn in like a lamb to the slaughter.

If I'd said "no" to Richard and walked to bank of the Potomac, it is quite possible that I would have avoided tumbling into the tumult that arose as I struggled to find out more about Zahide and probably I would've gone to dinner with Nadir and Leyla. We would've gossiped about Levent, and I would've gone back to my place, my home with Stray, no matter how late the hour. The next morning I would've gone to Pont, going on in my own way with the modest life I had made for myself. Zahide would've remained an item of news for me, a particularly distressing items of news but one that I was able to keep at a safe distance.

I would've calmed down as I sat on the bank of the river, realizing that I had overreacted to what Levent had told me. It would've become clear that me that I'd actually done well and that I have a tendency to exaggerate some things, as my therapists had pointed out. The Potomac would have rippled like the Sea of Marmara, and I would've seen the locals fishing on the banks of the sea as I listened to the waves, my head resting on the rail. Perhaps I would've convinced myself that Zahide was nothing but a figment of my own imagination.

As I hummed songs—I wouldn't have known whether they were hers or my own—I would've mumbled to myself that it was just a temporary loss of memory, possibly brought on by the side effects of the medication I'd been taking.

If I'd refused, I could've made a habit of hanging on to daily life, which day by day I had been learning to do. When I went shopping I would check the expiration dates and the nutritional value of the food I bought. I even kept up with current affairs. Over time, I had learned to hold my temper. For example, the way that the New Conservatives greedily sought more and more power no longer irritated me as much as it used to, because there was one thing I could see more clearly now: Power was the key word of the times. Everyone sought it, and when they laid hands on it, they'd exclaim, "Got it!" just like Leyla liked to say. I got along well with Ali and his family, and sometimes they even let me look after Stray. That may have only happened twice and for just a short time, but still it was something. Everything boded well. I was building up a social life, and had found that I could breathe in that new city and enjoy the campus life packed into its streets. I had a home, and the city reminded me of who I was. If I'd said no to Richard and walked towards the Potomac River, I might very well have resumed that parody of a life.

Perhaps my character brought me to my destiny. There I stood, in the midst of that tumult, trying to decide.

I went inside.

It truly was like an underground world, which could've meant many things. It was underground because they had everything you could possible imagine, everything.

I left Richard by the registers and wandered down an aisle.

The kitchenware area had an overwhelming assortment of items. As I made my way towards the clothing section, I was caught off guard by the fact that so many of the items were actually top-name brands. I surmised that the store was the final resting place for the belongings of reasonable democrats and hardened yet good-natured diplomats. There were silk shawls, candelabra, candles, almanacs, trinkets, vases, pencil cases, anything you could think of. One item, a ceramic vase, was particularly alluring, and when I saw that it was only two dollars, I decided I could indulge myself at least for that.

I was unable to drag myself away. I've always had a weakness for candleholders and candles, and soon my basket was filling up. And then there was an irresistible saxophone curio, and then a rather fancy lighter that I couldn't pass up.

In the clothing and accessories section, I found a pair of Timberland boots and a necklace, and I still hadn't even been through the kitchenware aisle or looked at the chairs.

"Were you able to find what you were looking for?" someone asked me from behind.

I turned around and found myself face to face with a man wearing a rather elegant military uniform.

As though I'd been caught stealing, I set my basket on the ground. Standing almost 6 foot 2, that soldier with his white ponytail turned out to be none other than Richard.

All I could say was, "Why are you dressed like that?"

"What do you think? Do you like it?" he asked, turning full circle like an aging ballet dancer.

"Sure. Well, I can't say that it's quite you."

"You can't find the uniforms they have here at any other store," he said.

"Well, I don't suppose many people go to secondhand stores to find uniforms, especially military uniforms."

"I suppose not," he said.

There was something strangely familiar about him as he stood there in that blue uniform.

And at that moment, all meaning seemed to fall away.

And then Richard began repeating a sentence with a ritual rhythm, and it was hauntingly familiar:

Per me si va tra la Perduta Gente

Per me si va tra la Perduta Gente . . .

The secondhand store seemed to shift under my feet and I felt like I was in space, on the verge of drifting off and losing everything.

No, my name couldn't be Emel.

I heard myself in Richard's voice: *Per me si va tra la Perduta Gente . . .*

There had to be more.

I wasn't Emel. The torture, the sorrows, and all the experiences I'd been through struck not at my body but at my soul, my very being, for the very first time.

Per me si va tra la Perduta Gente.

You are bound to me, Richard was repeating. Sohni, you're bound to me.

You're bound to the future

You're bound to live.

Bound to immortality.

You're bound to me, Sohni, I'm your God.

It all came back, and Emel was washed away as I remembered who I was: Sohni. It was all there, deep down in my memory. I remembered the days when I was Zahide. Like snapshots, like pictures in the weekend supplement of a newspaper, the images came flooding back. I remembered the Turkish lessons I'd taken. I remembered all the dead of the world, the birth dates engraved on gravestones. My immigration. Maryland. All of it. Like a film strip, accompanied by that worn out image, and that sentence kept running through my mind: "likeafilmstrip likeafilmstrip likeafilmstrip" with the vexation of a cloying illness;

and there, amidst the smell of blood, pus, sulfur, and spring days and the song "Sohni Remembered" accompanied by spice and music, I remembered: the long days spent in the house in Kensington, the stadium, Richard's soothing voice, his hostile voice, the electric shocks and my soul, the hypnosis—we used to do that when we were children, lookathewatchlookathewatchthenwewouldlaughoutloud—walking my children home from school, the instruments of torture, the planes, suicides, vileness, secrets. Then there were the people who had to be spat on and the others who didn't deserve it at all. There was so much that had been unnecessary. Then I recalled the military equipment, the hallucinations, Levent, my tiny cell. Then the stadium, that grandeur, and then my cell again, the way my echoing voice had become a nightmare. I remembered muttering to myself: "Issomeoneafraidofherself?" then the name Emel, the pool, our trips, the way I filled the jar of laughter for her, our parting, how I began to resemble her, the surgeries. Emel. I remembered enough. It was momentary, but enough to know that we can never find the life for which we search.

"Sohni," Richard said, "you'll never be able to find the life you're looking for."

He was obviously quite pleased with the situation.

"How about a little trip down memory lane," he said. "I can give your womb some of that old time pleasure. As much as a Muslim whore can enjoy it, that is."

We were in the middle of the store, surrounded by life's castaways, the belongings and clothes of people who had died or moved on to other places. Everything was a jumble, like a celebration of death.

"Let's enjoy life, day and night. Like we used to. Put on your best clothes, dye your hair with henna, darken your eyes with kohl and tell me about those faraway lands and your childhood again. Let me lie at your knees. Let me recreate you once again by ravaging the privacy of your body and bring you death yet again, that's what makes a whore so alluring. Come, let's enjoy immortality. Open your womb to me."

And with those words, everything came to an end.

That's where Richard met his end.

All it took was an imitation silver candelabrum. Even though he was much taller than me, I swung and it descended in an arc, thudding against the side of his head and he tumbled forward, knocking me to the ground and we became entangled in a mass of fabric and curtains as I struggled to get free. But it was as though we'd vanished from the sight of everyone there. I heard the rustle of his gabardine military trousers as he pressed his body against mine and then the sound of my stockings ripping as he grabbed at my legs. I pushed against him but under his weight I was helpless, and I felt him thrust into me as his white hair hung in my face. With sour breath he said, "You're mine, you cheap bitch" and I felt him explode inside me, penetrating my every cell with his seed. That's when I managed to get hold of the candelabrum again and finish him off. Who knows who it once belonged to. A diplomat perhaps, perhaps even an emissary from Turkey. For a moment I imagined him sitting at an elegantly laid dining table illuminated by candlelight. I was pinned beneath his stiff body, struggling to get out from under him. At last I was able to shove him aside and get up. And then I staggered and fell. I got up again, and swung again and again at his head; even in death he refused to die as his soul swirled with unknown ghosts, but in the end I managed to topple a television over him, and he finally he lay still. I was spattered in blood.

"Sohni, ascend one more level, one more, all the way up to heaven. Virtue is the vile degradation of a whore like yourself. Bathe in my blood. It is the grandest virtue that the world can offer you. Bathe and become purified, bathe and transform yourself. Become clean with this holy blood."

"Damn you to hell!" I shouted.

I looked around. I was surrounded by a group of people who stood staring at me in shock, muttering to each other in Spanish. I understood enough to know that someone said, "We should call the police." I was covered in blood and semen. Richard was lying on the floor, dressed as a retired soldier. We notice odd things at times like that. I saw that there was a set of the complete works of Shakespeare on a nearby shelf, including Richard III. The irony of it all. But the universal thing was blood. Not literature, not life. Just blood, eternal blood. As the white floor turned red with Richard's blood, the crowd surrounding me drew closer, seeming to loom up larger than life, a seething mass of huge amoebas. I saw fear in their faces. And everything in the store seemed to swarming in towards me as well, suitcases, underwear, safety pins, doilies, vases, toys . . .

Stand back, I heard someone say. Just like in the movies. A man was waving a badge, shouting at the crowd to move away.

Yet another preposterous scene, I said to myself. Sweat dripped from my hair onto my bare shoulders.

It was Levent. Or someone that looked like Levent. No, it was Levent. My hands were cuffed.

We proceeded through the crowd.

Levent?

As he held my head to his chest, he reassured the crowd that everything was under control. All I heard was background noise. Noise and a deep silence.

He pulled me towards the back door of the store. There were no police cars. There was no one. Just a one car, Nadir's Toyota Corolla.

I was bleeding and shivering.

Levent took off the handcuffs. He kept repeating, "You have to get out of here." And I asked over and over, "Who am I?"

"You'll get your answer. But now, you have to go."

Nadir asked where we should go.

Home?

"You have to go home and change out of those clothes and leave town right away," Levent said.

Nadir took back roads I'd never noticed before. Richard's blood, semen and sweat began to dry, his putrid breath and cursing slowly drying on my skin.

Nadir parked in front of the house.

We rushed into the house and I changed my clothes.

"Listen," Levent said. "I'll tell you everything, but first you need to leave town. Take the first train to New York and then catch a flight to Turkey. I'll meet you there in a few days. I'm going to give you a file that will give you the answers you've been looking for."

I stopped shivering.

"Are you a cop, FBI, Turkish National Intelligence? Who the hell are you?" I asked.

"I can't tell you that right now," he said. "All you need to know is that you have to leave. Now."

I had no idea what to say.

Soon after we left, but first I went to the bathroom. Ever since arriving in DC, I had been suffering from constipation, but at that moment everything broke loose. Nadir came to the bathroom door and asked if I was okay. They probably thought I might kill myself. When I came out of the bathroom I shouted, "To hell with both of you!" but they just shrugged it off. To be honest, I didn't want to be taken seriously. I didn't want to take anything seriously ever again. As I was packing up a few things I heard Stray howl. We decided it would be safer if I took a taxi. Levent repeated, "You'll find everything you need for your flight to Turkey in a mailbox in Madison Square. Here are the directions. Go there as soon as you get off the train."

I glanced at myself in the mirror next to the cabinet. The person I saw was me and not me. I'd had that sensation before, but never that strongly. I mumbled something to myself. A curse, a song, a riddle. Perhaps my name . . .

I murmured everything, I murmured nothing. I walked through the rooms of the house. Everything seemed to be in pursuit of nothing. As I paced, I felt the energy that is hidden in all the words in the world. I called out to myself, reaching out for the power in the universe, that which can transform you into a killer if you believe in something too strongly: "My God! Who am I?"

I walked out into the yard. Some lilies were in bloom.

"You're going to miss the coming of spring here," Levent said.

"How thoughtful of you," I thought to myself. "At the very least, you're good for something."

"Are you talking to me?" Levent asked. In fact he was caring, a truly thoughtful and kind person.

"You know about Zahide, don't you?" I whispered.

He nodded. "Yes, I do."

We left the house. For the last time, I glanced at the flowers blooming in the yard.

Classified.

URGENT

Phone no:...

Re: Rendition program--the CIA--countries in coopera-
tion with the CIA and torture.

Your Excellency, the following is a summary of the
report concerning the rendition program, especially at
the prisons involved in the rendition program. We urge
our government to take prompt measures on this issue.

Major General A. Y.

Within the framework of the rendition program starting
from the earliest phase, there have been numerous problems brought about by the fact that some detainees were
medicated and tortured in the countries to which they
were sent and then included in projects held underground
in stadiums in subcontractor countries. The entirety of
these incidents contravene the provisions of the United
Nations Convention against Torture, of which the USA is
also a signatory. A primary issue is the legalization

of torture by countries allied with the USA in their anti-terrorism efforts, and it has been noted that torture victims have been forced to sign statements under coercion. The article of the Convention is very clear: No exceptional circumstances whatsoever may be invoked to justify torture.

During the trip from DC to New York, I had read almost everything in that yellow file about Zahide when that telegram slipped out from the other documents. The date indicated that it had been sent quite some time in the past. That yellow folder that Levent gave me explained everything. And brought it all to an end.

I was renewed, reinvigorated. Revived. I was both Zahide and Emel and neither one nor the other. It was like growing up all over again, living out those painful years of adolescence when everything seems like a reproach. I felt that long ago I'd taken a train journey but something had been missing, and now I, as two people in one body, was bringing it to completion.

When I got off the train in Madison, it was five in the morning. It took me a while to find the mailbox Levent had told me about. I'd had fears that it would be empty, but when I opened it with the key that Levent had given me, I saw a large envelope. I found a secluded bench, sat down and carefully opened it. There was a Turkish Airlines ticket for a flight to Istanbul that evening, $250 in cash and a passport. The name in the passport was Öznur Şahin. My new name. And I saw that I had yet another new occupation: elementary school teacher.

18

August 16, Istanbul

For months, I'd been wandering idly in Istanbul with my new name and identity. Summer had finally arrived and whispers of autumn were already in the wind. I was living with an elderly woman about whom I knew nothing. We shared the basement floor of an apartment building in the district of Moda.

The streets seemed to reveal rather than hide the reality I wanted to escape from. That dusty city seemed to be filled with fall leaves blown in the wind. The puzzle had taken on another level of complexity, and I struggled to breathe and live as Öznur Şahin. Weary of reading and re-reading the file that Levent Koryürek had given me, I felt as though my head were a heavy stone that swung pendulously as I wandered Emel's Istanbul, getting lost in the labyrinthine streets of Moda, wandering in the bustle of the district of Bahariye. It was her city, and I was trying to make it my own.

One day, while trying to decide whether or not I should go to Adapazarı, something happened that eased my suffering. As I was getting ready to go out, my cell phone rang.

"May I speak to Öznur?" asked the person at the other end of the line.

"Speaking."

"Hello, Öznur, this is Levent Koryürek. I'm in Istanbul. We need to meet."

"Of course," I said, unable to conceal the excitement in my voice. "Where?"

"At Haydarpaşa," he said. "In the waiting area of the terminal that's next to the stadium. Tonight."

"Of course," I repeated.

When I arrived at Haydarpaşa, there was a breeze that seemed to be whirling around me, an autumn wind that blew ashore from the Sea of Marmara. It felt like a materialization of that curtain which had long eluded me, the curtain pulled by fate between life and death.

It was a quarter past ten and the station was crowded. I'd been nervous because I didn't want to keep Levent waiting. I made my way through the crowd, which made me think of the hordes that would descend on Judgment Day, and found my way to the waiting room. Despite my fears of being late, I was early. I waited for a while in front of the door, but didn't see him. Thinking that perhaps he was inside, I decided to go in. The clapboard door squeaked when I opened it, and as I stepped inside my nostrils filled with the smell of damp wood, reminding me of the smell of dorm rooms. There were only a few people inside, and they all seemed shrunken somehow as I approached the wooden counter in the rear of the room. I noticed that there was a young man with a slight mustache marking x's on a piece of paper, which I assumed to be a horse race form. Steam rose from a pot of tea boiling on a propane stove beside him, fogging up the window that over-looked the far end of the square. Beyond the steamed-up glass, there was nothing but night and the trains that looked dull and faded in the weak light which painted everything in the same wan hues. The young man with the mustache showed no interest in my presence. To get his attention I cleared my throat, but he didn't respond. I approached him and described Levent, asking if anyone who looked like him had come in. Without looking into my eyes, he nodded ambiguously and said "No." I waited a little longer in front of the counter. Then I slumped down on one of the chairs. The man sitting across from me turned to the woman beside him and said, "Don't worry, Mother. We won't have to wait long." She glanced around, her expression weary. "I'm not worried, Son," she said, "Too much worrying just causes trouble. All that matters is that we get there safe and sound." Her voice was timid, quiet. Aside from them, the only people in the room were an elderly man and a young couple. Everyone's heads were bowed, as though they had succumbed to whatever fate had laid out for them. I, too, felt that I would soon strike such a pose. Levent was still nowhere to be seen. My mind was filled with far-fetched scenarios explaining why he couldn't come, but I tried to brush them aside.

I suppose that I was still in the grip of those days and years that held me in captivity because I couldn't bring myself to just get up and leave. Even though I'd only seen him a few times in my life, Levent knew the secret that had cost me my entire existence, so I went on waiting.

"People who leave never come back, so don't wait in vain."

Emel had said that. She described America—which had driven me to escape—as the wrong place for me: "If there's still a place where you can return and live, go back. Don't waste your time here." That day was Thanksgiving. We'd had nothing but our mutual gratitude and friendship, and some turkey we'd bought in pre-cut pieces because it would be easier to cook. As I raised my glass to toast our friendship, she raised hers and said, "To our friendship and freedom." I didn't know whose freedom she was talking about, but the idea of freedom struck me as being so very alluring. The door opened and I snapped out of my reverie.

It wasn't Levent.

A frail boy wearing a hat came in, wheezing "Fresh hazelnuts!" As he peddled the small paper sacks of nuts, it occurred to me that he sounded as though he had bronchitis or asthma. He walked among the rows of chairs and then stopped in front of me. The yellow stripes of his green shirt were barely visible through the grime. He seemed far too young to be out in the night at that hour, and I noticed that he was shivering. With thin fingers, he picked up a paper bag from the tray, on which were scattered a few nuts. He bowed his head as he held out the bag, and I saw that his hat, which had a Wizards logo, was just as stained and dirty as his shirt.

"No, thank you," I said.

"Very cheap."

"No," I said.

"Very cheap," he insisted.

"Okay fine."

He handed me the paper bag and then fumbled for something else on the tray. I wasn't surprised when he held out a yellow envelope, the same color as the yellow stripes of shirt.

"This envelope is for you," he said. "Levent Bey asked me to give it to you."

The envelope was embossed with the logo of Pont. I opened it and found a rather official-looking document and the *Metro* supplement dated from two days before. I turned to that ominous page, and when I saw that picture of Richard's grinning face, my blood went cold. "Our beloved Richard Shelton, also known as Jan Gabriel, was a great journalist and writer and an exceptional person, my best friend. He passed away five months ago, and today would have been his birthday." There was also a short piece about Emel. "She came to our town as a visiting journalist and Pont scholar, and studied under Richard. Emel will always remain in our hearts as a guest of honor and be dearly beloved among us. Emel, who would have been celebrating her birthday two days from now, was sadly found dead in her house."

"Levent Bey apologized for not being able to come tonight. He said he'd try to see you another time."

"It's not important," I said.

"He said that something came up," he said and then sat next to me. But it was strange; he suddenly acted as though I weren't even there.

"Thank you," I said. I assessed the situation: A boy selling hazelnuts and the night lights of Haydarpaşa; an envelope on my lap, the *Metro* supplement, a paper bag of hazelnuts. Not a bad start to an adventure, I mused. Other than a few phone calls and a brief meeting with Levent, I hadn't really talked to anyone since I arrived in Istanbul. I had no one in my life. I was an unemployed teacher, nothing more. Just who was I, what was I? It was almost autumn, and while the days were unbearably hot, the evenings had a chill reminiscent of a high plain far from the sea. Everything was changing, and I couldn't keep up. I couldn't cry; I couldn't laugh. There was little I could do. I approached the man with the mustache and asked for a cup of tea. For a few moments, he pretended that he hadn't heard. Then he said, hesitantly, "Sure. We don't normally serve passengers, but this time I'll make an exception."

Later, I thought to myself: Why was he even there in the waiting room then? It made no sense, unless he was a spy.

I left the station and set about finishing my business which was, in short, the destruction of the stadium. I planted the explosives as carefully as I would arrange the houseplants in a home where I'd lived all my life. Then I slipped out, like a black snake, with no expectations for the future, leaving behind all that sin and evil in the halls of the stadium.

There's little else to say. The *Metro* supplement that Levent had sent brought me the message: Activate Mount Qaf, all the preparations are in place. Take action. To put it in proper terminology: Do whatever needs to be done. I placed the bombs at the base of that glorious heap of steel and concrete and set the timer.

Later, much later, I set my mind on going to Adapazarı.

The prayer-like murmurs of the old woman opposite me merged with the surprising course of an undefined day:

When will it come, when . . .?

And then there was the raspy breathing of the boy selling hazelnuts next to me.

Hanging on the wall opposite me, there was a faded calendar showing the month of August.

The squeak of the rear door of the waiting room.

The way my sandals slapped the floor covered on the worn-out carpet. Levent's failure to show up, the sealed lips of the past, the envelope in my hand, names. The name Jan Gabriel, which seemed to have drifted through my thoughts the entire day. It was a strange moment in which I waited for that desperate stretch of time. I heard a familiar tune as I sat there, feeling the weariness of the day like a weight in my body. I listened carefully. I knew that song. Did it really sound like her? The voice was too rich, too sonorous, to be an impersonation. It was Pervin Ferit, Sohni's mother. A chill ran down my spine, just like the first time I heard her ethereal music. A rhythm symbolizing love, annihilation, rebirth and reunion with the almighty Creator. Or perhaps it was simply a reflection of Emel's studies, which she dedicated so much of her life to. A name that her advisor had said, anger in his voice. Our shared destiny in which she trapped herself, one that would always take me to her or bring her to me. A voice: Pervin Ferit of the Pakistani Sufi tradition.

The young man with the mustache, that's who did it. The spy. The way he just sat there doing nothing made him seem like a spy. How should I know? But he played the tape of that song.

Undulating in the illumination of a bright fluorescent light, the song spoke of the story of a bygone love. *Ahki Gud-e-e-dekh-h*. Look at those eyes. My voice sang along with all the sounds in the room. Look at those eyes. And no one paid me any heed at all. That was a good thing. Only the boy by my side. He was the only one I couldn't get away from. He was still by my side, listening to me.

I wanted him to ask me how I knew the song. Then I could tell him all about my life. That would be counted as the beginning of everything. Maybe my goal wouldn't be to tell him about all my sorrows; I could begin by telling him that I was actually a good person. I could tell him how, while living as a good person, I had abandoned everything and rushed headlong towards hell. I would occasionally remind him that I didn't do it for my country or my husband. No, I had always been running away from myself. I could mention that he looked like my brother. Like yours, his shirts were always dirty when he was young. Like you, he had light-colored eyes when he was alive. He might say that mine were the same. Mine? What does that mean?

That's how we resemble one another, I could say. Then moving on to the song, I would come to the point. Emel listened to that song. No, it was another one of Ferit's songs but it sounded like that. She listened to it in Zahide's dorm room. Who's Zahide? you'll ask. Never mind. Emel heard this woman's voice in Zahide's dorm room for the first time. She asked me what it was about. But then she didn't want to know. Don't tell me, I just want to hear the music, she said.

Together, we listened to the music. That night, we listened to that song—I can't remember the title right now—on the cassette tape called "The Powerful Lose by Winning." We listened to it three or four times. We listened to "Eagles and Rats" in Urdu. What do you think it's about, I asked her. "I'd always thought that we listen with our ears," she said, "but now I know better." Ears are just an excuse, nothing more.

The boy by my side didn't ask anything.

If he'd asked, I would've told him, but he didn't.

I was going to ask him, do you know what "The Powerful Lose by Winning" means?

He didn't ask.

I opened the bag in my hand and began to eat the hazelnuts. Their shells were fresh, like slivers of thin formica between my teeth,

How did you know, Emel? Do you know Urdu?

Did I really know Urdu? Zahide, tell the truth.

Yes! Yes! Yes!

* * *

If we stayed any longer it seemed that our faces would turn the color of the waiting room, lounge, office or whatever it was. The train would soon pull out of the station. It was almost two in the morning. The boy had fallen asleep with his head on my shoulder. I gently nudged him and he woke up. He looked at me, his expression blank. "Let me come with you," he said. His name was Cihan. That's when I found out that Cihan was an orphan.

For people like us, what risk is there? I asked myself. We have no one else, we have nothing. We move from country to country, we change worlds, we change temperaments, minds.

"All right," I said to Cihan.
Cihan quietly looked at me and smiled.

19

After boarding the train, I read a document that was in the envelope Levent had sent.

July 2006, Pentagon

Dear Senator,

This is in response to the documents gathered by Mr. Koryürek and the explanations concerning them in the correspondence that you sent to us. I am not fully aware of how he conveyed this information to you, and therefore I felt that I should respond to you in detail. Mr. Koryürek works with the criminals in our rendition program and has been a part of the program team since day one. He was the head of a team of health specialists and as a military figure who led the medical team that kept track of Zahide Sohni Mühür in the rendition program from the beginning, I am distressed to hear about Mr. Koryürek's denunciation of our institution and Operation Erase Personal Destiny (OEPD). Mr. Koryürek's use of such exaggerated terms as "inhumane," "monstrous," and "unscrupulousness of the century" to describe the program is clearly unjustified. The person in question, Zahide Sohni Mühür, belonged to a terrorist organization through her husband. She and her husband lived in the United States with their two sons. Her husband was a family physician, and she was a dentist. They had been involved in underground activities in the country for ten years. However, the increasing pressure on Zahide Sohni Mühür by her husband, and her inability, or perhaps I should say refusal, to take on a more active role in the organization, changed everything. Approximately two years ago, she approached the FBI as a possible informant. She had left her husband and was on her own with her two sons. In the meantime, the Pakistani Secret Service stepped in. A house in Kensington, Maryland was rented for her. Of course, it was no ordinary house. It was located next to the residence of journalist Richard Shelton—one of the founders of OEPD. If you ask why, I would say we had to proceed with extreme caution due to the fact that we had discovered the existence of sleeper terrorists after 9/11. Mühür had numerous charges against her, and we had to proceed with extreme caution. During her time in the witness protection program, she unexpectedly contacted someone who had been released from Guantánamo and who was also in the witness protection program. As you well know, the legislation on this issue is explicit. When people are in the witness protection program, they have to shun contact with others, especially people who have been charged with the same crime. If they do so, the program is terminated. Even though the contact in question was her brother, Zahide Sohni Mühür made a serious mistake, and this cost her the lives of her two sons and her own freedom. After contacting her brother, which is when she attempted suicide which resulted in the death her two sons, we were the first to respond on behalf of the government. She was under close surveillance for nearly two months and given the necessary medication for her treatment. As a woman who had lost both her sons, she was given all the psychological support she needed. And then, under the terms of the rendition program, and in a way that would not unduly tax her, Zahide Sohni Mühür was sent first to Europe via New York, and from there to Syria. Following procedure, she was put back in the witness protection program and underwent plastic surgery so that she could live comfortably in society. In this way, she was given the opportunity to start a new life. She continued her life as a Turkish journalist, but unfortunately she was killed unexpectedly in an accident. The way that Mr. Koryürek described this process as contemporary Nazism is baffling. I think it is quite disrespectful for someone who played such a significant role in the creation of the OEPD to criticize the organization in that manner. To put it in his own words: "We may think that people only have one life, but that's simply not the truth."

In no way do we agree with the statement that "the administration of medications represented inhumane forms of treatment." The text sent to us which states that "especially within the framework of the rendition program, starting from the earliest phase, some detainees were given drugs and tortured in the countries they were sent to, in contravention of the provisions of the United Nations Convention against Torture, to which the United States is party" must be dismissed as unfounded. We proceed along the path laid out for us by the community of nations. In approximately two years, we are going to see the results of this treatment program. The fact that these people have been granted new identities and new world views is the crowning achievement of this project, in a sense the victory of our century, and the manner in which Mr. Koryürek slanders it demonstrates a personal weakness on his behalf.

The ideas proposed by Mr. Koryürek about the stadiums are nothing short of fiction. The appropriate people will get in touch with you to explain this matter and give you the answers you are looking for. However, I will say that we have launched a project that involves the use of stadiums, but not in the way described by Mr. Koryürek. Suffice to say that we have employed some of the top minds in the Muslim world in our A New World is Possible (NWP) Project. Mühür was among the first hundred people in the project, and therefore it is unthinkable that we would have physically tortured her as you alleged because there are strict health requirements in the NWP project.

OEPD, of which Mr. Koryürek was one of the founders, is a program in which the mind is transformed, not destroyed. During the process of transformation, the individual establishes a special connection with people in his or her past, as well as with the person administering the medications. In no way do we perceive it as a "master-slave" relationship as Mr. Koryürek puts it.

In short, this project aims at nothing more than the reintegration of criminals into society and we created this program on a semi-voluntary basis for the people of our country. However, we came to the conclusion that we should no longer use Americans in the program. Terrorism came to our rescue at this point. Transforming these terrorists, rather than keeping them incarcerated, became the founding principle of our work. Our government is not keeping secrets from the public. The following quote is from a press conference that was given by our Secretary of Defense to the international community: "The prisoners are sent abroad to be interrogated and to prevent them from further wrongdoing. This is not a one-way traffic and is not unreciprocated. We send the prisoners because we trust your governments and you send us their confessions. No one has any complaints about this." As for Mr. Koryürek's statement, "It was all for security intelligence, but everything ended up being a justification for torture," we would have to consider this an extremely emotional and partial point of view.

Nonetheless, I should state that our institution highly values the contributions that Mr. Koryürek has made. To date, we have collaborated with him on several projects. Moreover, we have taken many important steps forward together, steps that will benefit the government of his own country as well. In closing, Mr. Koryürek's denigration of a project that has been running quite smoothly is simply beyond our comprehension. As for the accusations Mr. Koryürek made about the late Richard Shelton, a neighbor of Zahide Sohni Mühür, we judge them to be of a nature unbecoming a man of science.

We wish you success in all your endeavors.

Respectfully,
Karen Blaster
OEPD Coordinator

20

In the early morning of August 17, the Adapazarı train slowly pulled out of Haydarpaşa station. As the cars of the train rolled onward, these words seemed to echo from their midst: *Per me si va tra la Perduta Gente.*

Mount Qaf Stadium had been given a voice and spoken at last.

Although it was still night, it seemed that the windows of the city glimmered in the sun. From massive loudspeakers affixed to the columns of the dark stadium which stood in arrogant grandeur between the sea and the distant barren hills of the city, strange words poured forth, followed by rumbling music. The sound first shuddered past the thick columns and flowed outward through narrow alleys towards the terminal and thundered along broad avenues that seemed to strike out, free of the towering stadium. There was something miraculous yet repulsive about the music, as though it had unleashed a dark spell into the world, a spell that whispered of love and death. The music spread forth, leaving in its wake a feeling of unease that was ever so slightly perceptible, like a layer of soot barely visible to the naked eye. Between the notes of the music lurked a bitter taste, a sharp smell like varnish and linseed oil that drifted unnoticed among the slumbering inhabitants of the city. And the people who were awake at the hour, exhausted by their labors, thought the smell must have come from a nearby furniture factory or perhaps from a fire that had broken out. That's what they assumed. That indescribable sound spread out towards the sea, the waves, the distant hills. In the end, it didn't vanish, but simply burrowed away in hiding.

And that's all it was, a music and a scent. But that wasn't the end.

A loud explosion was heard as the columns of Mount Qaf Stadium, groaning with the sound of the music, suddenly burst, sending forth a hail of debris that showered down like a spring rain, seeping and flowing over the shames of humanity.

And from that point on, everyone was guilty.

March 2008
Maryland–Istanbul